"Just when you thought it was safe to be single, along comes Ally Carter's sparkling debut. *Cheating at Solitaire* is fresh, funny and clever, clever, clever—I loved this book!"

—Alison Pace, author of *If Andy Warhol Had a Girlfriend*

"What a find! Ally Carter has a terrific voice and she deals out a read that's packed with heart, humor, and fun. *Cheating at Solitaire* is a sparkling debut! I couldn't put it down."

—Johanna Edwards, author of *The Next Big Thing*

"Dealing readers a hand filled with humor, fun, and a cast of quirky characters, *Cheating at Solitaire* is a sure bet for a good time."

—Jennifer O'Connell, author of *Bachelorette #1, Dress Rehearsal* and *Off the Record*

# Cheating at Solitaire

## Ally Carter

BERKLEY BOOKS, NEW YORK

**THE BERKLEY PUBLISHING GROUP**
**Published by the Penguin Group**
**Penguin Group (USA) Inc.**
**375 Hudson Street, New York, New York 10014, USA**
Penguin Group (Canada), 90 Eglinton Avenue East, Suite 700, Toronto, Ontario M4P 2Y3, Canada
(a division of Pearson Penguin Canada Inc.)
Penguin Books Ltd., 80 Strand, London WC2R 0RL, England
Penguin Group Ireland, 25 St. Stephen's Green, Dublin 2, Ireland (a division of Penguin Books Ltd.)
Penguin Group (Australia), 250 Camberwell Road, Camberwell, Victoria 3124, Australia
(a division of Pearson Australia Group Pty. Ltd.)
Penguin Books India Pvt. Ltd., 11 Community Centre, Panchsheel Park, New Delhi—110 017, India
Penguin Group (NZ), Cnr. Airborne and Rosedale Roads, Albany, Auckland 1310, New Zealand
(a division of Pearson New Zealand Ltd.)
Penguin Books (South Africa) (Pty.) Ltd., 24 Sturdee Avenue, Rosebank, Johannesburg 2196, South
Africa

Penguin Books Ltd., Registered Offices: 80 Strand, London WC2R 0RL, England

This book is an original publication of The Berkley Publishing Group.

This is a work of fiction. Names, characters, places, and incidents either are the product of the author's imagination or are used fictitiously, and any resemblance to actual persons, living or dead, business establishments, events, or locales is entirely coincidental.

PRINTING HISTORY
Berkley trade paperback edition / December 2005

Library of Congress Cataloging-in-Publication Data

Carter, Ally.
    Cheating at solitaire : a novel / by Ally Carter.
        p.    cm.
    ISBN 0-425-20574-6
    1. Single women—Fiction.  2. Women authors—Fiction.  3. New York (N.Y.)—Fiction.
    4. Tabloid newspapers—Fiction.  5. Self-help techniques—Fiction.  6. Actors—Fiction.
    I. Title.

    PS3603.A7765C47 2005
    813'.6—dc22                                                                    2005048002

PRINTED IN THE UNITED STATES OF AMERICA

10   9   8   7   6   5   4   3   2   1

For Mom, Dad, and Amy

# Acknowledgments

There are so many people who are responsible for bringing finished words to the page that it is almost impossible to acknowledge them all. There is not a doubt in my mind, however, that this book would not have been possible without Kristin Nelson, agent extraordinaire, who didn't have me committed when she saw how drastically different my second book would be from my first; I can't imagine a better partner for this journey. In addition, I'm tremendously grateful to Allison McCabe, an editor's editor, whose talent is evident on every page. Thanks also go to everyone at Berkley for their tireless devotion to the cause.

Julia has been in my mind for years, but it wasn't until Caroline and Nina came into focus that this became a story worth telling. For that, I owe both Beth and Vanessa, who have never committed a crime on my behalf (but would if I asked them to), and Mace, who would always be there to post bail.

Every writer needs great readers, so I am grateful to everyone at FOCL, who offered critical eyes when I needed them and a lot of laughs in between.

But most of all, I thank my family, who taught me how to laugh and how to work.

# Prologue

Julia was staying at the Ritz. Always the Ritz. Only the Ritz. Like a lot of women, Julia reserved a special place in her heart for the elegant restaurant where a man had popped the question that had changed her life. But instead of a Tiffany ring, Julia walked away that day with a two-book deal, and from that point on, Julia James could afford to buy her own diamonds.

Five years later, Julia had climbed fourteen stories from the hotel restaurant to a luxurious suite where the lights of the city shone through sheer curtains onto her unadorned hands. She flew quickly through a deck of cards and grew lost in the familiar motion as her mind drifted back to the day Candon Jeffries had told her she was going to become a star. At the time, Julia had nearly laughed at him. Ten pounds overweight and self-conscious about it, she considered herself to be a perfectly ordinary single woman. But Candon had worked side by side with Julia in the trenches of the publishing world, and he knew that she didn't sit at home on Friday nights, waiting for a boyfriend to ask her to the movies. She didn't live on microwave popcorn and bad takeout. Instead, Julia went to the movies alone. She froze individual servings of homemade lasagna and chicken Kiev and never thought twice about the phone that didn't ring. Julia James wasn't just another single girl in the city. She was, he declared, the queen of single girls—the Elizabeth the First of lower Manhattan—so he had proposed that Julia share her gift with the world. That lunch at the Ritz five years ago marked the point when Julia James went pro.

Now she was a guest of the Ritz, on her third trip, promoting her third book, waiting for her third ride to Rockefeller Center and her third conversation with Katie Couric. In the meantime, Julia was playing her billionth hand of solitaire. She could have played on the computer, but she liked the feel of a deck in her hands, the brush against her thumbs as she shuffled, the methodical, even motion of laying out a hand. Plus, Julia liked being able to cheat.

She tried to focus on the cards or the memory of the lunch—anything but the ominous ticking of the clock beside the bed. Four forty-five in the morning and wide awake, Julia pulled the cards together again and shuffled.

# Chapter One

"Good morning, Ms. James," the driver said, opening the door of the Town Car.

Sleep and fatigue crusted in Julia's eyes, and she had a hard time returning the smile he beamed toward her, brighter than the sun that was still waiting to bring day to New York City. Julia settled herself onto the plush leather of the backseat and said a silent prayer of thanks that the driver had worn a nametag. The face she recognized, but his name was lost among the myriad of others that floated through her subconscious like a fog. *Charlie,* she told herself. *Charlie. Charlie. Charlie.* She tried mnemonic devices:

*Charlie the tuna. Charlie's Angels. Charlie, the male Charlize Theron.*

"How are you, Charlie?" she asked once the man had settled himself behind the wheel.

"Well, I'm great, ma'am. And how are you this fine and beautiful morning?"

"I'm very well. Thank you for asking."

"We got early editions of all the papers back there for you. I hope you don't mind, but I peeked already and saw those books of yours are still on the bestseller list. Your folks must be awfully proud."

It was far too early in the morning for Julia to think about her mother, who had probably already scoured the paper and hung Julia's clippings on the refrigerator right next to her report card from the second grade. Instead, Julia picked up a paper. Breath lodged in her throat as she began at the bottom, scrolling toward mid-list where *Table for One*, her debut, was holding strong. Her second book, *Spaghetti and Meatball: Meals for the Single Person*, was just a notch or two above that, on the Advice, How-To, and Miscellaneous list. But as Julia's eyes returned to the main list and continued moving up, she soon stopped breathing completely. With every passing line, her heart pounded harder, until she crossed into the top ten and saw *101 Ways to Cheat at Solitaire* sitting there, staring back at her, proof in black and white that *life is good*.

They eased into predawn traffic, and Julia scanned the streets around her. The city's support staff was already hard at work, like the backstage on Broadway, making sure the props were placed and the lighting was perfect. Beer trucks lined up in front of bars. Laundry vans skirted restaurants. Storeowners washed windows and rearranged displays. Julia watched the world put on its makeup, comforted by the fact that even the greatest city in the world has morning breath.

Charlie was looking at her in the rearview mirror. His knowing stare was enough to make Julia wonder if she had lipstick on her teeth or had missed a button on her blouse.

"I tell you, Ms. James," Charlie said finally, "I see your author photo all the time, but you're even prettier in person."

Relief flooded over Julia as blood rushed to her cheeks. People sometimes told her she was pretty—one even went as far as to say she was beautiful—but, Julia admitted, her mother was probably biased.

"I hope you don't mind my saying so, ma'am," Charlie went on, "but you just get prettier every year."

Bright red now, Julia didn't know what else to do, so she said, "Why, thank you, Charlie," and turned to look out the window.

"You sure do have some fans," the man went on. "I'm sorry to say I haven't read anything of yours. But my sister, she's a big fan—forty-six and not a man in sight. Yep. She's a *big* fan."

Julia was staring out the window at Fifth Avenue, thinking about the opening scene of *Breakfast at Tiffany's,* remembering why, for a short time, New York City had been her kind of

town. Not because it was the sort of place where you can
window-shop in formal wear at five A.M., but because it was
the kind of place where you can do that and trust that no one
will stare.

"So, you've got a new book out now, I guess?" he asked her.

"That's right."

"Well, I'm going to have to get one for Lou Ann." Charlie
cocked his head and grinned. "She reads those books of yours
and talks about how she doesn't need a man. And it's a good
thing, too, 'cause she sure doesn't have one."

They reached the studio, and despite the damp morning
air, tourists had already lined up outside the *Today* show's
windows. Charlie pulled the car to the talent entrance and
got out to help Julia with her door. A cry rose up from the
crowd when she emerged from the car, but Charlie quickly
stepped between Julia and the masses, shielding her with his
broad body. "You be careful out here. Some of these women'll
get ya."

Julia chuckled and pulled a fresh copy of *101 Ways to
Cheat at Solitaire* from her bag. She scribbled inside and
handed it to Charlie, who looked down at the book in his
hands as if he were staring at a block of gold. "Oh, Ms. James,
I wasn't fishing for a . . ."

She squeezed his arm. "It's not for you. It's for Lou Ann,"
Julia said with a wink, then stepped away from Charlie and
the car, turned and gave a big wave to the masses, and slipped
through the studio entrance.

♣

*This can't be good,* Julia thought as she sat next to the tiny and adorable Katie Couric. Katie always looked trim and petite on TV, but it wasn't until Julia saw her in person that she remembered how truly waiflike the anchorwoman was. Julia did the mental math. *If Katie looks like this in real life, and like that on TV, what am I going to look like on TV?* She straightened up, sucked in her stomach, and suddenly wondered why she cared.

"Now, the new book is called *101 Ways to Cheat at Solitaire.* Isn't that right?" Katie asked.

"Yes, it is. I love playing cards, Katie. I carry a deck with me everywhere I go, so when I was discussing themes for my next book with my longtime friend and editor, he pointed to my purse and said that the answer was right in there. I guess he was right."

"Your first book is a staple on the bestseller lists. You followed that with a cookbook, *Spaghetti and Meatball: Meals for the Single Person,* and that further broadened your fan base. How do you keep moving forward? Keep the material fresh?"

"Well, Katie, all of my work deals with helping single people cope in a couple's world. In *Table for One,* I wrote about how it doesn't have to be scary to be alone. With *Spaghetti and Meatball,* I wanted to help single people tackle common challenges, like shopping and cooking for one in a family-sized world. With *101 Ways to Cheat at Solitaire,* I have taken a huge, and for some women very *intimidating,* concept—the idea of being single for the rest of your life—and broken it down to a manageable size, one hundred and one easy things that every woman can do to thrive as a single person."

Katie shifted and rested her chin in one perfectly manicured hand. "So, how does Julia James cheat at solitaire?"

"I'm a thirty-four-year-old single woman, Katie. And I'm happy. I don't believe happiness is reserved for those who are dealt great hands. Happiness is a decision you make—a goal you work toward. And when life doesn't give you the cards you need to win easily, then . . ." Julia cocked an eyebrow as a guilty expression flashed across her face, "it's time to cheat."

Katie shifted. "You were listed as one of the ten most bankable writers in America. How does that make you feel?"

"Blessed." Julia waited a beat and then added: "And rich."

They laughed their way into a commercial break.

Lance Collins woke up to the sound of the ringing phone, although he couldn't imagine that he'd even been to sleep. He picked up the receiver, dropped it immediately into the cradle, and tried to return to the comfortable place on his pillow. But again the phone rang, so he rolled over and answered it.

"Hello," he said, groggy.

Sunlight streaked through the dingy window and horizontal blinds and fell across the rumpled sheets that tangled around Lance's legs. He fought to straighten himself as he heard an unfamiliar female voice ask, "Lance?"

"Yeah."

"It's Tammy."

"Who?"

"Tammy at Poindexter-Stone. You know, great eyes. We got Thai food one night," the woman named Tammy went on, irritation rising in her voice. But in his current state, Lance wasn't sure if he could remember his own mother's eyes.

"Oh, hey, baby," he said, realizing too late that the "baby" might have been too much.

"Save it," Tammy snapped. "You're late. I know. I'm calling to remind you to take your head shots."

At this, Lance swung his legs to the floor. "Take them where?"

"Are you still in bed?" Tammy shouted, forcing Lance to hold the phone away from his ear.

Lance looked at his feet on the floor. Technically, he was *on* the bed, not *in* bed, but Tammy with the great eyes and the love for Thai food probably knew bs when she heard it. Tammy probably had a BS in bs, so he didn't argue.

"I can't believe you're blowing this off!" she jabbed at him.

"Blowing what off?" Lance shot back.

"You got a call for Wesley Star," she said, her tone resonating with "duh."

"First I've heard of it," he said.

"I left you a message," Tammy said, as if her efficiency had been offended. Call her baby. Forget her name. Do any of a number of things, but don't accuse her of being unreliable. That was where Tammy at Poindexter-Stone drew the line.

"Well, I never got a . . ." He looked at his answering machine with its blinking red light and yelled, "Shit!"

"Be there by nine fifteen, and don't forget the head shots," Tammy said and hung up without a good-bye.

◆

When she left the studio, Julia got a cab. The publishers had offered to have a car at her disposal while she was in New York, but hailing a cab was the most quintessentially Manhattan thing she could do, and she wanted to do it as much as possible before she had to go home to Oklahoma for Cassie's birthday.

"Where to, lady?" the cabbie asked, and Julia loved the sound of it. *Ah, New York,* she thought. *It's good to be back.*

"The Ritz," she answered, and the car pulled away from the curb.

♠

According to Lance's agent, the mysterious Wesley Star was a casting agent who held the key to the city of starving actors and, one by one, decided who would get out and who would go home with a bus ticket paid for with Western Union money. Wesley also decided who would keep waiting—the unfortunate few who had just enough talent to remain in permanent limbo.

Finally, Lance thought as he pushed the elevator button, he was going to meet the mysterious Wesley and, he hoped, step a little closer to the gates. But like his career up until that point, he ran up against a brick wall as soon as the elevator doors slid open.

Chaos filled the hallway. Young, athletic action-hero wannabes leaned like bookends beside middle-aged men who looked custom-made to play "Accountant #3." The noise of actors practicing lines pinged off the tight walls and crashed against Lance, nearly pushing him back into the elevator with cries of Hamlet and Tennessee Williams. It was either the offices of Wesley Star or the waiting room at the insane asylum—at that moment, Lance wasn't quite sure which.

"Lance," a familiar voice said. He felt a tug at his arm and turned to see a face he had seen at every audition he'd been on in the last ten months.

"Hey, Tom," Lance said, glancing at the paunchy man, remembering to feel both guilty and grateful that God had granted him naturally straight teeth and a better-than-average metabolism. He looked quickly away, toward the mayhem of the hall. "This is crazy," he said.

"Yeah," Tom said. "Wesley is going into semiretirement, so no one knows how many more open calls the dude's gonna have."

"Open calls?" Lance said, remembering Tammy's emphatic insistence that she'd pulled off some amazing favor on his behalf.

"Well, yeah. I mean, they've requested some people, but Wesley's famous for walking through the hall, seeing a face he likes, and making history." Tom shrugged slightly and turned as the elevator doors opened and another man stepped out, trying to squeeze his way through the crowd. "I'm not gonna miss this," he said. Then, seeing Lance's dazed expression, he explained: "I'm going west in three weeks."

"Yeah?" Lance asked. "Things going that well for you?"

"Well," Tom said, and Lance thought he recognized the tone of a so-so actor who had the sense to know he was also a so-so liar. "Not really. But I've been hopping at the Ritz and the tips are good, so I can afford the move."

"Really?" Lance asked.

"Yeah."

"The Ritz?"

♣

"Welcome back to the Ritz, Ms. James. I trust your accommodations are acceptable?" the manager said as Julia approached the desk. Just the way he stood there, serenely perfect and ready to serve, made Julia consider challenging him to a round of a little game she liked to call Ridiculous Ritz Request. She'd never had the courage to play out loud of course, but secretly, she wondered what would happen if she asked the pristine man behind the mahogany counter to find her something outrageous—maybe a ferret in a fedora. How long it would take for him to round one up? Knowing the Ritz, she guessed he'd be knocking at her door in less than an hour, ferret and hat in hand.

*Tempting*, Julia thought, but decided to ask for her messages instead.

"Of course, ma'am, a package." He removed a small brown envelope and handed it to her across the counter. "Will there be anything else, ma'am?"

"No." She eyed her mother's handwriting on the address label. "This will be all," she said just as her cell phone started to ring. She turned from the counter and strolled across the immaculate lobby while she dug in her purse for her phone.

"You were on TV," a little voice exclaimed before she'd even said hello.

An immediate smile lit Julia's face. "Was I really?" she teased.

"Mommy and Grammy and Nicky and I all watched you!"

Julia didn't have to strain to imagine her niece's serious expression as she explained the facts exactly as they were. Cassie was a genius, Julia was sure. She was also the perfect child. So pretty. So sweet. In fact, if Julia hadn't been present at her birth, she would have sworn the little girl had been purchased at Pottery Barn.

"Well, how did you like seeing me on TV?" Julia asked.

"It was okay," Cassie said, giving it serious consideration. "But I like you being here better."

"You know what?" Julia asked, homesickness creeping into her gut. "I like being there better, too."

Then Julia heard a scuffle followed by static and finally Caroline's breathless greeting. "Julia?"

"Yes?" Julia said, drawing out the word, waiting for the shoe to drop, certain that her sister wouldn't have taken time from the dishwasher/ironing board/vacuum cleaner trifecta that swallowed her days like the Bermuda Triangle unless there was a favor in her future.

"Well," Caroline's voice dropped to a barely audible whisper. "As you know, someone has a b-i-r-t-h-d-a-y coming up, and—"

In the background, Julia heard Cassie cry out, "I'll be this many!" She imagined her niece holding out a plump little hand with five splayed fingers.

"Well," Caroline continued, "she saw something on television about FAO Schwarz, and now she's just dying for something from there—her words, not mine. Dying for it."

"We've created a monster," Julia said.

"No, big sister, you created this particular monster. I'm just the one who has to feed and clothe it twenty-four hours a day. Anyway, since you're there . . ."

"Okay," Julia said, cutting Caroline off before she could cross through the doorway marked *Danger: Sleep-Deprived and Underappreciated Nursing Mother Ahead—Proceed at Own Risk*. "I'll see what I can do," Julia conceded. "Kiss the munchkins for me."

"Do it yourself on Saturday," her sister replied.

"Gladly." Julia hung up the phone and turned her attention to the package. Inside the envelope was a printout from the

Web site of the fabulous FAO Schwarz. It had careful red circles around a half dozen items.

"She really is a monster," Julia said to herself, then slipped the piece of paper into her purse and dropped the envelope in the trash. She got into the elevator and went up to her suite to change.

When Lance's name was finally called, he was escorted into the office by a woman whose manner made it clear that whatever appeal actors had ever held for her had worn off years before; experience in her business was like Kryptonite for hunks. In this woman's presence, even his best smile was worthless. Instead, Lance had learned, efficiency was what she valued. If you show up early, have your pictures out of the envelope and ready to hand over, and you don't waste her time, a little bit of her will love you forever.

She took the pictures he offered. "Strip to the waist," she said, choosing, he surmised, to show her affection on the inside.

Lance started taking off his shirt. "Who will I be reading with?" he asked.

The woman slipped on a pair of very thick glasses and said, "You won't be."

"Then shouldn't we wait for Wesley?"

"He's not coming. You do nude?"

"Excuse me?"

"Do you go buff for bucks?"

◆

As the cab came down Ninth Avenue, Julia checked her lipstick in the rearview mirror and locked eyes with a man who
looked as if he didn't care to be reminded that cosmetics existed. As if she'd just offered to give him a tour of a hot-dog
factory, the driver's face said that while he might enjoy the
finished product, he really didn't want to know how it gets
that way.

She put the lipstick back in her purse and double-checked
to make sure she had her lucky pen, although the event at the
bookstore wasn't going to be a big deal—that was the idea.
Candon had suggested she do an intimate book signing at a
small, independent bookseller she had loved during her copy-
editing days, so ever the class kiss-up, Julia had agreed, almost
asking if any of the faculty needed her to stay late and dust
erasers while she was at it.

It was a little thing, Julia told herself. Virtually no publicity. She should be in and out in an hour or two, with very little
fuss. Honestly, Julia was starting to wonder if it would even be
worth her time. But when the cab turned the corner at Fifty-
second Street, she could tell she was going to need a plan B.

At least two hundred women stood outside the bookstore
windows. She thought that maybe Hollywood was filming a
Brad Pitt movie or some plastic surgeon was inside handing
out free Botox. Perhaps Burberry was giving scarves and um-
brellas to the masses to promote their new *anyone and their*

*dogs can wear us* marketing campaign. Seriously, for a second Julia didn't know what could be causing all the fuss. Then she realized that the fuss was for her.

"Um, excuse me." She leaned close and spoke to the driver. "Do you think there's a side entrance we could try?"

"No way," the driver said. "Crazy lady meeting here today. You the tenth crazy lady I drive here. They all want to go away from the other crazy ladies. I sorry."

"You don't understand," Julia said. "I'm the crazy lady." She reached into her bag, pulled out a copy of *101 Ways to Cheat at Solitaire,* and turned to her picture and bio on the back cover. "See," she said, pointing to herself. "Head crazy lady. Really, it's okay. I can go in the back."

"Fine. I take you to the back," he said, then added as if Julia couldn't hear, "crazy lady."

# Chapter Two

When Lance reached the office of Poindexter-Stone Talent Agency, he was hit with a wave of déjà vu. The crowd was far too reminiscent of his experience at Wesley's, and this time, he was in no mood to stand in line.

Tammy had her great eyes glued to a glossy magazine and was ignoring the multitude of starving future stars who filled the chairs and lined the particleboard walls. She kept the phone in the crook of her neck as she expertly cruised through the ringing lines: "Poindexter-Stone, please hold. Poindexter-Stone, please hold. Poindexter-Stone, please hold."

Unlike the woman at Wesley's, Lance suspected that flirting might still work with Tammy, so he thought about Thai food and eased himself onto the corner of her desk.

"Save it," she snapped before he'd said a word.

"I've got to see Dick," Lance started.

"Don't call Richard Stone 'Dick' if you want to work again."

"Like I'm working now?"

Tammy seemed to accept this as a valid point, and Lance wondered if she was an actress herself. She seemed actress-ish— kind of pretty, a little surly, and as if she hadn't eaten enough to fill herself up in at least three years.

"Well, he's not here," she said, as if the matter was completely out of her hands. Not since Pontius Pilate had someone so completely passed the buck.

"Well, what are we going to do about it?" Lance asked.

She flashed a patronizing grin and gestured to the overflowing room. "You could sit."

Lance glanced back and shook his head. "Not good enough."

"You could call," she said and gestured at the ringing phone covered with blinking lights.

"Don't you think you should answer one of those?"

"If it's important, they call back," she said with a flip of the magazine's pages.

"Fair enough." He got off the desk, sunk to a knee, pulled her bony hand into his, and said, "Tell me where he is."

"No."

"Oh, come on," he pleaded. "It'll save me a lot of time and you a lot of hassle. Come on, just a little hint."

She sighed, looked around at the other actors in the waiting room, then leaned close and whispered in Lance's ear: "Lunch. Stella's. You didn't hear it from me."

Lance kissed her cheek. When the phone rang again, he answered for her: "Poindexter-Stone, please hold."

♠

Julia liked Stella's on Seventy-fifth because they knew her there. Not in the "Hey, you were on TV so I should kiss up to you" sense. They knew her in the same way her father was known at her hometown coffee shop in Oklahoma. No big deal in Fall River, but Julia believed that sort of thing should not go unrewarded on the Upper West Side.

In a word, Giovanni, the maître d', was surreal. He never forgot a name or a drink; he remembered birthdays because once, on that date, your friend had slipped you a card and paid for lunch. He asked if you'd enjoyed the sea bass on your previous visit, and if you felt up to trying the salmon today. He noticed when you cut your hair.

He was smart and attentive, with a sexy little accent and easy access to excellent food, so if Julia hadn't been so happy being a writer, she might have tried to help the single women of the world in a different way. She might have tried to clone Giovanni.

"Oh, Miss James!" He met her at the threshold, took her hands in his, and kissed both her cheeks. "You come back to Stella's! It's been too long. I see the reservation in the book and I pray it be you!"

"Hello, Giovanni. It is wonderful to see you, too."

"I see in the book that we are two for lunch today. Is that so?"

"Yes," Julia said as he helped her remove her coat and scarf.

"Is it, by chance"—he cut her a sly look—"a man? Someone special?"

Julia mentally rolled her eyes as she remembered that Giovanni was one of about three people in the world who still tried to set her up. "Yes, Giovanni, he's my agent, and we have a very special *professional* relationship." She didn't go on to say that Harvey was sixty-four with two great passions—food and a wife of forty-one years.

"Oh," Giovanni said, not trying to disguise his disappointment. "At least it will not break my heart to see such a beautiful woman dining alone. Your table is ready. Come."

He led her through the small dining room to a prime table, motioned to the water and bread boy, then excused himself, reminding Julia of why he was the perfect man: He'd known exactly when to disappear, but not before offering $H_2O$ and carbohydrates.

Three tables away, two men were finishing their meals. One man stooped low to the table and spoke while his companion ate in slow, even bites. "I think you could use another pair of hands," the talker said. "You've got more clients than you can handle. I've got more clients than I need—and none of them any good. You've got good people and I've got good contacts. What do you say? Want to hang out a shingle?"

The other man motioned to his eggplant. "I'm in the middle of a meal."

"I know, I know. You need some bread. Here, let's get you some bread."

Almost every table was occupied in the noon-hour rush as waiters in long, white aprons scurried around, carrying baskets of bread and plates of pasta. The rich, decadent aroma filled the small dining room and seeped onto the street outside, where Lance Collins stood formulating a plan, watching his agent on the far side of the room. He saw Richard Stone turn and scour the room for someone or something. *He might as well be looking for me,* Lance thought as he mustered his courage and started inside. But he'd hardly passed the threshold when the maître d' stepped in his way.

"May I help you?" Giovanni asked.

"No thanks," Lance said. "I see the person I'm looking for." He moved to step around the little man, but Giovanni slid quickly into Lance's path.

"Oh." Giovanni smiled, still studying Lance but seemingly with a new objective in mind. "You are Miss James's agent?"

"No," Lance said, stepping forward only to be cut off once again.

"You have a reservation?" The tone hardened.

"No, I told you. I'm meeting—"

Giovanni stopped smiling. "Miss James is meeting an agent. Mrs. DiAngelo is meeting a daughter. You are no agent, and you are no daughter. You must leave Stella's." He had a hand on Lance's arm and was steering him toward the door, and Lance felt opportunity slipping through his fingers. With one last look at Richard Stone, he grasped for inspiration.

"Representative!" Lance yelled.

Giovanni's grasp on his arm loosened, so Lance carried on, "I don't like the term *agent*," he said, as if he hated to be a stickler for such things. "I prefer *representative*."

With that, Giovanni studied Lance, and then he brought both hands to the side of his face. "You are a friend of Miss James?" he asked.

"Oh, yeah," Lance said. "A close *personal* friend."

A giddy grin flashed across the man's face, and he took off through the tables. As Lance followed, he began to worry what he was going to say or do when they reached this woman called Miss James. From across the restaurant, he saw a woman sitting alone at a table, studying a notebook. Lance found himself staring at the graceful curve of her neck and the way her red hair swept across her shoulder. He was instantly glad to be getting an introduction. Then he remembered that they were already *close personal friends*. He put his hand on Giovanni's shoulder and stopped him. He pulled a rose from a vase on a nearby table and spoke low in Giovanni's ear: "I can take it from here."

Giovanni turned to Lance and said, "Oh, it is a beautiful

day!" When he turned and went back to the entrance, Lance realized he was standing alone in the dining room holding a damp, stolen rose and looking at the kind of woman a normal man would probably only approach if he was drunk or on a dare. Behind her, he saw Richard Stone at his table in the back. He could just walk past her, Lance decided, but a glance behind him warned that the maître d' was watching his every move. Maybe men made a habit of coming there and trying to pick up women who were out of their league? Maybe he was just the latest in long line of suitors to go down in flames, and the little man at the door didn't want to miss the show. . . .

At the back of the restaurant, a waiter cleared Richard Stone's plate.

It was then or never.

Lance shook the excess water from the stem of the pilfered flower and slipped into the chair across from the woman called Miss James. "Excuse me," he said, and the woman looked up. "I don't mean to impose, but do you see that man over there?" He motioned to the two men in the back of the room.

"Yes," she said, drawing out the word as if considering the possibility that she might be on *Candid Camera*.

"Well, I really need to talk to him, and the only way the guy at the door would let me in here was if I said I was meeting you. I lied. I'm sorry. You're probably thinking that I'm a terrible person, and you're probably right. But if I could just sit here long enough to keep your boyfriend at the door from getting suspicious, then I'll go talk to that man and you'll never have to see me again. I promise."

Julia surveyed him. "I'm quite fond of Giovanni, my 'boyfriend at the door.' "

"And he's fond of you, too." Lance sat up taller. He gave her a toothy grin, but she didn't budge—not even a smile. He eased to the edge of his chair. "Anyhow, I'm sorry to bother you. You've been great. Really, very nice. Enjoy your lunch."

He got up and moved slowly, with cautious, backward steps, toward the men. When he saw the rose still in his hands, he tossed it casually to Julia, watched her catch it, and then turned to speak to Richard Stone.

"Richard?" Lance asked, feigning surprise. "Well, this *is* a stroke of luck, running into you like this!" He eased casually into a chair at the table and glanced at Richard's companion. "Hey, how ya doing?" he asked before turning his attention back to his agent. "So, I've been thinking about the types of auditions I've been going out on—"

Richard put a hand out, stopping Lance. "Do I know you?"

Lance looked at Richard, and then at the other man, then choked out a nervous laugh. "This guy," he said to Richard's companion while he pointed to his agent. "Seriously, Richard, I've been—"

"Seriously. I don't believe I have ever laid eyes on you before in my life."

Lance sat, shocked and confused, as he tried to process this one-sentence slam on him and everything he'd ever wanted.

That was his career, or lack thereof, summed up in a single sentence by a man with marinara sauce on his tie. "I'm Lance Collins. You're my agent," he said feebly.

Richard laughed and said to his companion, "I'm his agent. I'm supposed to get him *Hamlet,* and I don't even know who the hell he is." He turned to Lance. "Call my office. Make an appointment. I'm eating my lunch."

But Lance didn't leave. At that moment, he wasn't even sure his legs still worked.

"Look, kid," Richard said. "It's not me. It's you. Everybody's got talent. And you're a good-looking kid, but you can buy looks. Name recognition—now that's the honey. You can't put a price on that. You go get yourself famous, and then we'll talk about the kind of roles you want."

Lance knew there was a cliché about carts and horses, but he couldn't remember how it went. Luckily, Richard's companion chose that moment to wipe his mouth and ask, "Were you just sitting with Julia James?"

Lance looked back at the woman who sat alone, scribbling in a notebook, and said, "Yeah. I guess."

Richard emitted a little squeal. "Hey, kid, why didn't you say so? That's *great*! I mean, that's off-the-charts fantastic. How long you been seeing her?"

"Oh." Lance looked from Richard to the woman and back again. "You've got the wrong—"

"*I* say what's right and wrong," Richard corrected. "And believe me, this is right! Hey, who needs *Hamlet*? We've got

*Taming of the Shrew*." Richard laughed at his own cleverness. "Whatcha waiting for?" Richard asked. "Tell your girlfriend to come over!"

"You've got the wrong idea. She isn't my girlfriend."

"Not your girlfriend?" Richard asked as if this were a kink in his master plan to take over the universe. "Who knows?"

"Who knows what?" Lance asked.

"That you're here with her," Richard said, growing impatient.

"I'm *not* here with her," Lance insisted.

"If nobody knows you're not, then you are," Richard said, flipping his hands like a magician who had just made a quarter disappear. "You're here. She's here. A few tasteful photos and—"

"This was a mistake." Lance stood and left the table.

As he headed to the door, he passed Julia and heard her on her cell phone saying, "You can't make it? That's fine. I just hope you get to feeling better. Take care of yourself. Bye-bye." As she hung up, she looked at him and asked, "How did it go?" But the expression on his face must have been answer enough because she said, "That's a shame."

She'd placed his pilfered rose in the vase on her table. Water spots still darkened the linen tablecloth, but it seemed to Lance as if it had been a year since he'd joined her there.

"I'm sorry," she said, no doubt sensing that Lance hadn't enjoyed his time on the other side of the room.

"Thanks anyway," he told her and walked away.

♣

Was it the entire basket of bread that Julia had eaten or the morose look on the man's face as he turned and walked out of Stella's that caused her to lose her appetite? She honestly didn't know. But since Harvey, her agent, wasn't feeling well and wouldn't be joining her for lunch, Julia laid some bills on the table and went to say good-bye to Giovanni.

Two free hours felt like an unexpected blessing. She could window-shop or people-watch in the park—theater of the living, she'd always called it, and Manhattan was its greatest stage. But when Julia stepped beneath the restaurant's awning, a cool, wet wind slapped her across the face. Rain pelted the sidewalks, and pedestrians darted past like darkened blurs with newspapers and briefcases held overhead. Definitely not people-watching weather. On the street, traffic crawled, so Julia shivered beneath the awning, remembering that sudden thunderstorms always produced a shortage of taxis in Manhattan, while dry weather led to a bumper crop—the very opposite of rain's effect in Oklahoma. Shivering, she considered going back inside to finish her meal when she glanced behind her and noticed she was sharing the shelter of the awning with the same man who, moments before, had shared her table. An awkward pang flashed in Julia's gut, but the rain grew harder, and she wasn't eager to brave the weather and walk away.

*Do I know him?* Julia found herself wondering. He didn't seem like someone who worked in publishing, and she hadn't exactly been a social butterfly during the years she lived in Manhattan, but she couldn't shake the sense that she'd seen him somewhere before—maybe on a Wheaties box. Tall and strong, with sharp, gray eyes and broad shoulders, he had a clean-scrubbed, fresh-faced, All-American Quarterback way about him. She saw him cross his arms—strong, agile, hunky arms—and she thought she might be right, but then he caught her staring, so with the customary grace of every gangly girl who has ever been caught staring at the captain of the football team, Julia jerked her eyes back to the street. *Where's a bathroom to hide in when you need one?*

When at last a cab did pull to the curb, they both stood awkwardly for a second before she nodded at him and said, "It's yours."

"No," he said, shaking his head. "Take it."

"Really," Julia said and gestured toward the waiting car. She gave him her best "I'm an independent woman who appreciates the gesture but is happy to decline" nod, but the young man took her arm and led her out into the rain, opened the cab door, and once she was inside, closed it behind her.

Julia suddenly felt out of her element. "Where to?" she heard the cabbie say, but her eyes never left the man who had turned up the collar of his jacket and was lumbering down Seventy-fifth Street, a dark silhouette in the gray shower. "Lady," the driver said impatiently, drawing her back to the task at hand, "where are we going?"

"FAO Schwarz," she told him, and they pulled away from

the curb. They drove slowly, trying to meld back into the heavy traffic, so the pace of the cab matched the pace of the young man who hunkered against the wet wind. *It looks really cold out there,* she thought. *Pneumonia weather.* A shower of guilt washed over her. It violated her every feminist notion to take the only available taxi in New York when it was pouring rain. Plus, her mother would have told her it was rude. She cracked the window and yelled, "Stop!" When the cab halted, she cracked the window wider and yelled to the dark, wet figure on the sidewalk by the car. "Hey, come on. Stop."

He looked at her, and Julia no longer saw a cocky quarterback who was concentrating on the big game. Maybe it was the way the rain ran through his hair and streaked across his face, or maybe it was the way he slouched, hands in pockets, as if the weather was the least of his problems, but Julia said, "Come on, share it with me."

Lance looked up at clouds and reached down to open the door.

As they pulled into traffic and disappeared down Seventy-fifth Street, Richard Stone bolted from Stella's, climbed into a chauffeured Town Car, and yelled, "Follow that cab," as if he'd been waiting his entire life to say it.

# Chapter Three

"We still going to FAO Schwarz?" the driver asked. Julia and Lance looked at each other. Before Julia could respond, Lance said, "Wherever you're going is fine with me. I don't have any place I need to be."

"Are you sure?"

"Yeah," Lance said. "Go on," he said to the driver, then turned to Julia and eyed the toy advertisement in her hands. "Your kids must be crazy about you."

"Oh." Julia glanced at the laser-printed page. "No. I don't have kids. It's my niece's birthday."

"Oh, that makes more sense. That looks about right for an aunt."

"True." She laughed, and Lance thought he'd never seen a face so pure. After three years of looking at artificial lips and eyes and breasts, he felt like he was seeing genuine features for the very first time. "It's my job to spoil them," Julia admitted.

"I'm Lance Collins, out-of-work actor," he said and offered his hand. "Thanks for the lift."

Julia reciprocated. "I'm Julia James, person who buys the love of children."

Lance laughed and said, "No harm in that."

"So what happened back there? Who was he?"

Lance opened his mouth to reply, but Julia quickly waved her hand. "No. Never mind. That's none of my business."

"That's okay," Lance said. "That was my agent. He . . . well . . . we're experiencing creative differences."

"I'm sorry," she said.

"Don't be. You did your part."

When the taxi stopped, Julia handed the driver some money and told him to keep the change. She and Lance slid out of the backseat of the car, and Julia extended her hand again and said, "It was nice meeting you. Good luck."

"You, too," he told her. Then, instead of hopping back into the cab, he began walking down the wet sidewalk through the still-heavy drizzle. Julia stood in the plaza in front of the store's main entrance and watched him. *What if he's suicidal?* she thought to herself. *What if he walks in front of a bus?* Julia imagined waking up the next morning to a headline about a depressed, out-of-work actor who'd thrown himself on the subway's third rail. If that happened, she'd never forgive herself.

Then she looked through the glass storefront at a busy, public place filled with stuffed things and snappy music. "Do you want to come shopping?" she found herself calling after him. "Toys? Games? Lots of happy childhood memories? It might cheer you up." Lance looked back at her. Then, with the exuberance of a child, he said, "Cool," and led the way inside. As they stopped to admire a towering display, they didn't see Richard Stone staring at them through the window, hands cupped around his eyes.

"Oh, this is honey!" Richard muttered, then began dialing his cell phone. "Tammydonotputmeonhold!" he yelled. "Listen very carefully, and do exactly what I say."

Lance hadn't been able to see over the pile of toys in his arms for several aisles. Bright colors bore down all around them, and in the distance, the sounds of children playing superhero filled the air. He couldn't imagine that there was something in the store Julia hadn't bought yet, but they kept walking.

"*All* of this is for your niece?" he asked.

"I have a niece and a newborn nephew. Cassie is turning five on Saturday."

Her high heels tapped out a steady beat on the tile, and Lance marched dutifully behind, kind of enjoying the balancing act he was performing with an Etch A Sketch that teetered on top of the pile. "I hate to disappoint you," he said, "but some of these seem a little advanced for a five-year-old."

"You don't know Cassie. She's five going on forty."

"Ah"—he nodded—"one of those."

"Yes," Julia said, tucking more boxes beneath her arms.

Lance was beginning to think that he could get used to being around someone so comfortable in her own skin. *That's the problem with the theater,* he thought. *Everybody's acting.*

"So," he asked, trying to sound casual, "where's this party going to be?"

"Tulsa, Oklahoma. That's where I live."

"You don't live here?" Lance asked, a little dumbfounded and surprisingly disappointed. "Wow. I never would have pegged you for a tourist."

"Oh." Julia was quick to correct. "I'm not. I used to live here—years ago. I come back for business every now and then. You might say I'm more like an expatriate."

"Well," Lance said, mustering up a smile. "Welcome back."

"It is you!" a woman squealed behind them and ran through the aisle of toys, dragging a little boy behind her. Judging from the look on the child's face, Lance guessed that his arm was about to pop right out of its socket, and would have if the woman hadn't stopped in front of Julia.

"Miss James! Miss James! Oh, it is you! I'm Linda. Linda Westerman Worthington. I've read everything you've ever written. Everything!" The woman jerked the little boy's arm and said, "His sorry SOB of a father ran off and . . . Oh! I can't believe it's really you."

"Hi," Julia said, with her most professional smile. She leaned down to the little boy. "And what's your name?"

"That's Conner," the woman said offhandedly. "When I saw you standing here, I said to myself, this is fate! My story would be *perfect* for your next book. We could write it together. *One Hundred and One Ways to Disembowel a Cheater,* or maybe—"

"I don't do case studies. I'm sorry," Julia quickly jumped in, cutting the woman off. "Maybe a psychologist?" she added, patting the woman's hand. Lance thought the woman needed to be a patient of a good shrink rather than a coauthor. "Thanks for coming over. It's always nice to meet a fan. Have a nice day," Julia said and started down the aisle.

They'd almost turned the corner when the woman cried out, "Young man, when you're finished with Miss James, I need a few—"

"Excuse me?" Lance asked.

"I know you're busy now, but if you could just tell me—"

"I'm sorry, Linda," Julia said. "I'm afraid he doesn't work here."

The woman's eyes grew wide. Her gaze shifted between Julia and Lance, and her jaw went slack.

"Linda," Julia asked, "are you okay?"

"You're . . ." Linda said, pointing at Julia. "Here with . . . ?" Her finger trailed upward to Lance's perfect smile. "Come on, honey," she said, tugging her son's arm again. "Momma needs to go lie down."

"No offense," Lance said to Julia after the woman had disappeared into the next aisle, "but your fans are kind of weird. Does that happen to you a lot?"

"Trust me, toy stores are some of the safest places I can be. Now, video stores, grocery stores, airports—they can get pretty tricky. The downside of fame." Then, with a smile, she added, "Get used to it."

"I'd love to have the chance."

◆

Richard couldn't get over the size of it—really. He had wasted a few minutes worrying that he was having Tammy call in the wrong favor for the wrong occasion, but when he saw a man walking down Fifth Avenue carrying the biggest camera he had ever seen, Richard knew this guy could get the job done. Sure, it was going to cost him a Broadway audition for a private detective who couldn't carry a tune, but just one glance at that telephoto lens made Richard Stone start to salivate.

Once or twice, he started to go into the store and see for himself what was going on in there, but he stopped. He didn't want to scare them away. The money shot would come outside the store—the happy couple smiling and laughing after a shopping spree on the town. So he waited.

The rain had stopped, so pedestrians skirted the sidewalks, and, momentarily, Richard worried that there would be too much activity on the street to get a clean shot. But again, he looked at the size of the camera, and he knew he was working with a professional. Then, through the revolving door at the front of the store, Richard saw a mass of bright red curls waving in the wind that swept around the plaza. Richard said, "That's her. That's her. Get ready." The photographer steadied his camera like a sniper.

But wait. Something was wrong.

Where was the kid?

Did she ditch him inside? Richard was starting to panic. She was getting away. His master plan was crumbling. All the kid had to do was walk outside and stand next to her; how hard could that be?

He watched her ask the doorman to hail a cab, and Richard felt his heart fall to the pit of his stomach. She was going to get away. *Damn him*, Richard thought, and fought the temptation to run through the lanes of traffic and plant a kiss on her himself. Then Lance Collins walked out of FAO Schwarz, his hands full of shopping bags and an enormous bear tucked under one arm. Lance grinned, and as Julia James took the big bear from his arms, Richard noted that he really was a good-looking kid.

Instantly, snaps and flashes filled the air.

Richard pranced along the sidewalk, speaking to pedestrians like a vendor at a fair. "The name is Collins, Lance Collins. And he and Juila James are very much in love!"

# Chapter Four

Whenever Caroline was in a hurry, there always seemed to be a line at the neighborhood market. Luckily, Nicholas was sleeping comfortably in his carrier, and Cassie was scanning the headlines that bordered the checkout aisle. Caroline sometimes worried what effect exposure to tabloid headlines might have on her daughter, a sponge who absorbed everything she saw. But instead of worrying, Caroline decided she should just be grateful that her five-year-old child was gifted enough to be reading at this age at all. Plus, it occupied Cassie while Caroline kept a sharp eye tuned to the register.

"Excuse me," she said as the teenybopper in the blue smock whisked the cereal box over the scanner without a second glance at Caroline, who thrust a tiny slip of paper toward her. "I have a coupon for that," she said, forcing the coupon into the girl's hands.

"Momma," Cassie said behind her.

"Not now, sweetie. Momma's busy. Those are two for one." She gestured at the boxes of mac and cheese.

"Momma, it's Aunt Julia—with a boy!"

"Sweetie, don't say that. That might hurt Aunt Julia's . . ."

Caroline turned to her daughter and came face-to-face with a newsstand full of variations of the same picture—Julia and a handsome stranger, smiling on a New York street, their arms full of toys. A dumbfounded Caroline stared, mouth gaping, as she found the word to finish her sentence: "reputation."

Julia spent the first part of her morning on a Ritz treadmill. When she finally made it back to her suite, it was half past nine and the message light on her phone was blinking. Also, her cell phone showed eight new voicemails. *Eight?* She didn't think she'd ever in her life had eight messages at one time. Her first thought was for her family. *What if someone was sick or hurt?* She reached to call her sister, but as soon as she gripped the phone it rang, and the caller ID showed Nina was checking in.

"Weren't you even going to tell *me*?"

The sentence was so abrupt, so unexpected, that Julia might have wondered who had called her by mistake if Nina Anders hadn't sounded like a chain smoker since the second grade. No one on earth could impersonate her well enough to fool Julia.

"Hello to you, too," Julia said, a little put off with her best friend.

"Don't you change the subject on me! Who *is* he?"

"Who is who?" Julia asked.

"The hunk!" Nina yelled just as Julia flipped on the TV and saw her own smiling face staring back at her. First she saw her book's jacket photo, then some news footage of her making the media rounds, and finally, a scene from the day before as she left FAO Schwarz, Lance Collins trailing dutifully behind. Julia fumbled with the remote control and turned up the volume in time to hear the anchorwoman say, "The popular author and aspiring actor are all the buzz in the entertainment industry. No word yet on how they met, but spokespeople from the Collins camp do confirm that the couple is deliriously happy."

Lance woke up in a good mood. There had been some big tippers at the bar the night before and, for the first time in a long time, it looked like he was going to make rent without any help from his mother. He crawled out of bed at ten forty-five and checked his messages. He pressed "play" and listened to the automated voice tell him, "You have thirty-two new messages."

*What the* . . . Lance thought just as Tammy's voice came blaring out of the speakers. "Lance, it's Tammy. I just want you to know I'm fine with it." A long pause, and then, as if berating herself, she snapped, "Never date an actor! Anyhow, Calvin Klein is sending some clothes for you, and we'll have a car there to pick you up at five. Bye." *Calvin Klein clothes? Car service?* Then he heard the next message.

"Hey, stud. Richard Stone here. Martin and Steven just called looking for you, champ. Everyone wants Lance Collins! You're the hottest ticket on two coasts, kid, so give me a call on my private line." He gave the number.

The messages played on, one right after the other, each a little more surreal. If they hadn't referred to him by name, Lance would have sworn that the phone company had made a mistake. But no. People he didn't even know kept calling him *darling* and *sweetheart* and *champ*, and there was no surer sign that somehow he'd made it big in show business.

A banging drew him away from the machine. He unbolted the door and opened it, revealing a team of people who gave the words "high fashion" a whole new meaning. There was a man who was so tall and thin and dressed so elaborately that he reminded Lance of Mr. Peanut, all that was missing was the top hat and monocle. Flanking him were three women dressed in black who wore their hair pulled back so tightly that they looked like victims of botched face-lifts.

"Well," Mr. Peanut said, "do we have our work cut out for us here?"

He pushed into the apartment, his sirens in tow, and the four of them began undressing Lance, running fingers through his hair, inspecting his hands and nails. Meanwhile, the messages just kept playing. Amid the chorus of strangers pretending to be friends, Lance heard one voice he recognized.

"Mr. Collins. Julia James here. We . . . no, strike that. *You* have a big problem. Expect a call from my attorney."

"Attorney?" the fashionable man said. "Do I hear prenuptial?"

The women squealed, and then they pounced on Lance like lionesses on prey.

# Chapter Five

"Now, darling, relax. We're on this. It's taken care of," Candon Jeffries soothed, but Julia didn't sit. She paced the conference room and ignored its palatial views. The Manhattan skyline had never held so little appeal to her. All she could think was that Lance Collins was out there somewhere, loose in the city. He had used her like a scratch-off lottery ticket, trading her in for fifteen minutes of fame, and Julia wanted to make sure he wouldn't get a minute more.

"Come on," her editor went on. "Sit down. Drink some tea. Relax."

"Relax!" she yelled in a voice so high that she was lucky the windows didn't shatter and fall thirty-six floors to the street below. "I'm supposed to relax? My face is plastered across every sleazy rag in the country, with me looking like the world's biggest hypocrite! I can't believe you'd offer me tea. Do I look like I need caffeine? Plus"—Julia softened, sank into a seat at the table, and felt tears rush to the surface—"it's a really bad picture. I've got this whole"—she motioned to the makings of a double chin—"thing going on. "I look like a hypocrite. A *fat* hypocrite with a shopping disorder."

Candon slid into the seat beside her, saying, "I think it's a wonderful picture."

"Where's Harvey?" Julia asked abruptly. She picked up her cell phone and held it toward the windows as if there, in the middle of Manhattan, she might not have a signal. "Has Harvey called you?"

"I'm sure he'll call."

"I want my credibility back, Candon. I want it back, and I want it back now."

"We don't know it's been damaged. Let's look at the numbers and see."

"I don't care what the numbers say." She stood and slammed the newspaper, photo up, onto the table in front of him. "A picture's worth a thousand words."

Lance's eyes were starting to adjust to the dark shades that he didn't dare take off. He'd passed no fewer than ten news-stands, each one overflowing with pictures of him and a woman he barely knew. After the third person congratulated him on "getting some of that," he'd darted into a market and bought cheap sunglasses and an I ♥ NY baseball cap. But even in the elevator alone, Lance couldn't remove his disguise. He didn't like the person he'd become overnight. That morning, his grin was on every newsstand in America, but Lance didn't feel like smiling.

The elevator doors opened to reveal the usual purgatory outside the office of Poindexter-Stone. Eager actors lined the walls, so Lance pulled the cap lower and turned up the collar of his jacket and tried to bolt toward the door, hoping to fly by so quickly that none of his compatriots could aim and fire. He wasn't ten feet away from the elevator when he heard the first whoop.

"There he is, the man of the hour."

"Way to go, Lance!"

"Don't forget the little people, man."

"Does she have a friend?"

Lance should have had a smile and a comeback for each bit of locker-room banter, but all he could think of was reaching the door and strangling Richard Stone. He hurled himself into the office, slammed the door, and pressed his back against it as if trying to stem the tide of "atta boy" that flowed from the other side.

Tammy must have called in sick, or quit, because she wasn't there. If not for the calendar on the wall, Lance might have sworn it had been twenty years since he'd last set foot in that room. Everything looked a little bit different and a little bit the same, especially the woman who was on the phone, reading Tammy's magazine, looking exactly like the receptionist's future self. Unlike Tammy, this woman bolted to her feet at the sight of Lance, sliding her office chair back so quickly that it rolled into the table behind her and knocked over a stack of foam cups and left a pot of thick coffee sloshing like toxic sludge.

"Oh!" she stuttered. "It's you!"

Lance quickly glanced at her left hand. No ring. This woman was single and, he guessed, a Julia James disciple. *How*, he wondered, *were women taking the news that their crown princess was off the market, thanks to him?*

He eased toward the woman and took his cap off, for politeness' sake. The sunglasses, however, he kept on. "Is Richard here?" he asked, not quite recognizing his own voice, as if he'd somehow put a disguise on that, too.

"Where is he? Where's my golden boy?" Richard Stone virtually leapt into view like a Broadway extra—the only thing missing was the jazz hands. "Come here, you beautiful boy. Is this kid photogenic or what?" He pulled a tall stack of newspapers from her desk, and holding one toward Future Tammy, he asked, "I mean, can this kid take a picture? Look at those teeth. What do we have here—braces, caps?" He stepped toward Lance and tried to look in his mouth like a trainer inspecting a Thoroughbred.

"I need to talk to you," Lance said, slapping Richard's hands away.

"Great," Richard said, oblivious to the tension in Lance's voice. "Gotta strike while the iron is hot. Glad to see you get it." He stepped toward the filing cabinets and the hallway behind them. "Babe," he said to Future Tammy. "Hold my calls."

Richard Stone's office was surprisingly clean. If it had been two days earlier, Lance would have taken that as a sign of professionalism, and he would have ignored the mayhem of the hall and the lobby. He would have convinced himself that his career was going somewhere. But in the last twenty-four hours, he had developed the perspective he needed to see Richard and his office for what they really were—sparse and empty.

"Take a load off." Richard walked behind an enormous desk and sat down. But Lance didn't take the seat in front of him. He didn't move at all.

"Your legs broke?" Richard asked, impatience creeping into his voice. "Sit."

Lance stayed standing. "Whatever you started yesterday, you need to find a way to stop it."

"Excuse me?" Richard asked, jerking his head like he'd had water in his ears and hadn't heard correctly. "What did you say?"

"They're lies. Take them back," Lance said, growing stronger.

"Take them back? I hate to break it to you, Romeo, but this isn't second grade."

"She's a nice woman," Lance shot back. "We shared a cab and bought some toys, and now she's suing my ass!"

Richard stood, but with his small stature, standing behind the enormous desk made him appear even less powerful. "Are you growing a conscience on me?" he cried. "It's a tuna-fish world, and I'm offering you filet mignon, and you're growing a conscience?" He held up a stack of movie scripts and shuffled through them like a deck of cards, flashing the cover sheets as if asking Lance to pick a card, any card. "You see the names on these? You see the parts I have for you?"

The roles and projects that passed before Lance's eyes were, in a word, legitimate. Not B-level films or infomercials. Far better actors had started with far less. It would take one, just one . . . Lance felt himself reach for a script, but then he snapped back into the moment. "It's over. No deal."

"You don't even know her," Richard cajoled.

"Uh, yeah," Lance snapped. "That's kind of the point."

"This is America. Land of the tabloid. Home of E! Entertainment Television. There's no such thing as bad publicity! She owes you. You"—Richard pointed a Vienna sausage–shaped finger at Lance—"owe me."

When Lance turned to leave, Richard yelled out, "I can get you a baked potato to go with that steak." Lance took another step. "You're doing her a favor."

Lance wheeled and yelled, "You don't even know her!"

With eyebrows raised in the ultimate portrayal of irony, Richard said, "Neither do you." He sank back onto the throne of Poindexter-Stone and continued. "A buddy of mine in the book business just called. Her stuff is flying off the shelves, single-day sales records all over the place. Rumor has it they're gonna ink a seven-figure deal this afternoon. All because of our little project."

"I don't believe it!"

"Oh, believe it," the little man said. "Thanks to you, she's Cinderella."

The temperature had dropped, and the weather forecasters predicted that a late-spring snowstorm could blow in overnight. But when Julia wrapped a scarf around her head, it was as much to keep hidden as to keep warm. She pulled her hands into the hot-pink mittens Cassie had given her for Christmas, so when her cell phone rang, she had to struggle to flip the tiny device open and say hello.

"Julia?" the soft voice asked, and she almost couldn't make out her own name amid the noises of the city.

With her hands cupped around her ears, she replied, "Yes?"

"Julia, dear, it's Francesca." Then a mental image popped into Julia's mind to match the voice on the phone. *Harvey's Francesca*, the delicate, beautiful woman who had been her agent's world for more than forty years.

Julia darted into an apartment building alcove, ignored the stares of the doorman, and listened closely.

"Dear, I got your messages. . . ."

"Francesca, I've got to talk to Harvey. Could you . . ."

"No." Her response jolted Julia. "No, dear, that's why I'm calling. Harvey's in the hospital."

*Hospital?*

"He went to get the paper this morning and had a heart attack at the newsstand."

Shock forced Julia against the wall. She leaned against the glass doors, not caring about the mitten print she was leaving on the pristine glass. "Francesca"—she stumbled for words— "I'm so sorry. Is he . . ." *How do you ask a woman this about her husband?* Julia wondered. "Is he . . ."

"He's resting. The doctors say that's what he needs after surgery. No visitors," she added quickly. "By the way, dear, congratulations."

"Oh, Francesca—"

"It's a lovely picture. Harvey was clutching a copy when . . . the paramedics saved it for him."

*When this is over,* Julia thought, *I'm going to need a very good shrink.*

Back on the street, Julia began a list of reasons she shouldn't walk in front of a bus. Harvey wasn't a young man. In a city full of walkers and joggers and yoga-ers, she'd seen him break a sweat while heading to the bathroom. It was ridiculous to think that *she* had caused his heat attack. Then she rounded a corner and passed a newsstand, and her own heart nearly stopped beating.

Her cell phone rang, and she opened it quickly, anxious for news.

"Hi." It was a voice she recognized immediately. *Surely he wasn't calling her. Surely no one in their right mind had given Lance Collins her private number.* "Hello?" he said. "I was calling for Julia—"

"There is no way you are calling me."

"We need to talk."

She snapped the phone shut.

On the street in front of the Ritz, there were no reporters in sight, but Julia sensed them lurking like zits under the surface of her skin. She quickened her step almost to a jog, then she slowed instinctively. The last thing she needed was a picture of her running in pumps on the front page of the next day's papers, the headline: JULIA JAMES RUNS TO LOVE! or DON'T HURRY LOVE! or STOP IN THE NAME OF LOVE! The potential plays on words were endless. She wasn't about to give any pun-happy junior editor an easy gem to print in eighteen-point font.

She made it inside and to the elevator, and pushed the button. *Button lights up; this is good,* Julia thought. *Elevator doors open, good. Turn left. Fumble with key. Not good—who created these cheap little plastic card things? Red light. What does the red light mean?* She tried the card again. Another red light.

A door behind her opened and closed. A voice cried out, "Oh, my goodness!"

*A fan*, Julia thought. *Of all the times and all the places . . .*
She plunged the card into its electronic lock once more.

"I heard the news and I . . ." The woman behind her struggled for words. "It's just . . . you've always meant so much to me and . . ."

Red light.

". . . new hope. Such an inspiration. I mean, if *you* can find love, then *anyone* can."

*Hey!* Julia forgot about the lock momentarily. *I think I'm offended*, she thought, suddenly feeling like the Quasimodo of the self-help section.

She knew she should begin a one-woman PR campaign in the hotel hallway, but at that moment, all she really wanted was to be on the other side of that door.

"I'm sorry, but . . ." she started, when, to her amazement, she felt the door handle turn, opening from the inside. Stunned, she turned and came face-to-face with Lance Collins.

Lance grabbed Julia's arm and pulled her into the room. "I'm sorry," he told the woman, who dropped her Saks Fifth Avenue shopping bags where she stood. "We need a little alone time."

With the door closed behind them, Lance was squeezing Julia into the corner of the room. It reminded her of how her father would squeeze baby calves into the side of the corrals while he gave them shots. "Get close," he'd told her. "Don't give them room to kick." *Lance Collins must be a farm boy*, Julia thought. She didn't have a spare inch to move, much less enough space to haul back and kick him with her sensible shoes. He had one hand pressed firmly over her mouth as he spoke in a low, even tone.

"I know you hate me," he said, bright eyes staring into hers. "But we need to talk. Talk now—hate later. Okay?"

All she could do was look, wide-eyed, into his face and wait.

"Okay," he went on, "the hand is coming off now."

He slipped his hand away from her mouth, gently releasing the pressure until she was able to free her lips. She didn't scream. Instead, she bit—hard. *Let the man be the one to scream for once*, she thought, gratified by the sound of his yelp.

"I can't believe you did that!" Lance moved away from her and studied the red semicircle that surrounded the knuckle on his pinkie.

"Why?" Julia pushed past him. "Because you know me so well?"

"Hey, look," he said, following her, jerking his hand as if to start the blood flowing again to his finger. "I've got this agent. You know, the jerk from the restaurant. And he saw you there and, well, I didn't know anything about it."

"Do you want money?" Julia asked in her snippiest tone. "Because I have money. I can give you money."

"No," he said, stepping forward.

Julia stepped back. "Contacts?" she guessed.

"I don't wear contacts."

"I mean I can *get you* contacts. To help your career."

"Oh! I don't want your contacts."

"So you just ruin people for the fun of it?" she snapped.

"I assure you, I don't," Lance said.

"You're ready to clear things up then?" Julia asked. "Make a statement? Set the record straight?"

"That may not be the best thing for you," he answered.

"You know nothing about me or what's in my best interest!"

"I know you make little check marks when you buy things off a list. I know you're crazy about your sister's kids. And that you take lemon in your iced tea."

"Well, I never . . ."

"And I know you've got the number-one and number-two books in the country today." He reached into his pocket and handed a piece of paper to her. "This was under your door."

Julia recognized the Eli-Winter logo at the top of the stationery. Dumbfounded, she scanned the numbers while Lance put ice on his swelling finger. The handwritten note was in Candon's writing.

*Jules, I came by but you were out. Great news:* Solitaire *and* Table for One *are flying off the shelves—#1 and #2! The cookbook's way up, too. We've got to talk about what it means. There might be more room to spin it to our advantage. Dinner? I'll see if Collins and his people can come, too. Lots to talk about. Congratulations. CJ.*

*It can't be*, she thought. *It just can't be.*

"Are you okay?" Julia heard Lance's voice. It was close and full of compassion.

"Get out!" she roared and pushed him toward the door, growing stronger and more forceful with every step. "Get out of my room. Get out of my life." She grabbed the door, threw it open, and gestured for Lance to leave.

"Julia, you've got to believe me—"

"You have two seconds to get out of my sight!"

Lance didn't budge, obviously thinking that her instructions didn't apply to him. "Julia, listen to me," he pleaded. "This isn't my fault."

"Oh? Whose fault is it?"

Behind her, the elevator doors opened, and Julia heard Candon laugh and another man say, "It's honey." She turned to see the agent and editor coming down the corridor, smiling and laughing like old fraternity buddies.

"Now, this is a good-looking couple," Richard Stone exclaimed. "We can sell this!"

Julia glanced back at Lance in time to see a look of supreme shame cross his face. He sidestepped the two men and went to the elevator. When the doors opened, he stepped inside, and Richard Stone rushed in beside him. Julia was glad to see the doors slide closed.

"Sweetheart, you look wonderful!" Candon said.

"What's this?" She shoved the handwritten note in his face as he leaned down to kiss her cheek.

"Isn't that amazing?" Candon beamed.

"You want me to *lie* to my readers?"

Candon looked at her, confused. "I want to help your career."

"Candon, my career didn't need any help. My career was just fine. It was *my* career! Not yours. Not his. Mine!" She poked him in the chest. "You're going to fix this, Candon. Do you hear me?"

"Why don't you talk to Harvey. . . ."

"Harvey had a heart attack, thanks to this!"

Shock flooded his face. "Really?"

"This charade has officially crossed the line!"

"Julia, with the money we're making, you can buy Harvey the best doctors in the business."

"Was that a joke?"

"Julia, we don't want to stop this," he said simply. "Do you have any idea how much more you're worth now?"

She stared at him. In that instant, Julia realized Candon Jeffries didn't believe in her message—or in *her*. Candon believed she appealed to a demographic that had high disposable incomes and a lot of Friday nights to stay home and read. As long as there were lonely women, Candon Jeffries was going to try to sell them happiness in a bottle. Julia felt nauseous, realizing that for five years, her face had been on the label.

"I never want to see you again," she whispered.

"But Julia . . ."

Julia tried to retreat back into the safety of her hotel room, but the door was locked again. And she didn't even have the little plastic key. She turned and pushed past Candon, toward the elevators. When the doors parted she jumped in, and he followed. She jabbed the "L" button and watched as the lighted numbers descended while he quoted every valuable statistic in the publishing business. With every passing floor, he droned on. They'd had twenty talk-show requests, ten offers for couples books. Five new Julia James fan sites had popped up that day alone, each one proclaiming her a role model, an example, the new ideal.

Each one worshipping a lie.

When the doors opened into the lobby, she wrapped her coat around herself, pulled on her mittens, and rushed for the doors and the street. She forgot about the stupid potential headlines and ran. Lights flashed. Reporters yelled. "Julia, when's the big day?" "Julia, who's designing the dress?" "Julia, what's the next book going to be about?"

"Julia." This voice she knew. "I've got to talk to you."

"Lance!" a reporter cried. "Let's get a picture of you two together!"

Julia raised one hand above her head in an emphatic gesture. Irritation boiled over as she noticed her mitten-covered fingers and yelled, "I'm flipping you off!"

The mob thundered closer, and Julia was desperate for a cab, a quick escape.

Standing on Fifty-eighth Street, she could feel the cold wind through her wool coat as night began to fall on New York City. Then the flashes started, fast and bright. She couldn't see a thing. She swirled, lost inside the swarm of paparazzi, when a figure lurched between her and the predators. "Stop it!" Lance yelled. "Leave her alone."

Another flash came, closer, so bright that it made her eyes
burn. An abandoned luggage cart sat on the sidewalk, and
Julia took shelter behind it, but the photographers closed in,
pinning her there with no escape. Desperate, she grabbed a
makeup case from the luggage cart and swung it at the offend-
ing light. She heard a crash and a crunch like breaking glass.
Feeling the rhythm, she swung again and again.

# Chapter Six

"I am a good person," Julia said, half slurring her words, feeling them in her mouth like cotton candy, sticky and sweet and evaporating by the second. "I go to church. I'm kind to children. Then one day it rains, and I let a strange man share my cab. The next day, I'm a felon."

The clock on the wall above them ticked, its sound ominous through the hollow police station. Beside her, Lance shifted. "Hey! I wasn't the one throwing the Samsonite."

A tall man in a blue uniform came to stand before them then, his long shadow shielding Julia's face from the fluorescent glare of the lights above them. "Mr. and Mrs. Collins—" the officer began.

"That statement troubles me on so many levels," Julia said. "I am not married to this man. I am not engaged to this man. I cannot even stand the sight of this man."

The officer closed his file and said, "You sound married to me. Anyhow, seeing as this is more of a lovers' quarrel than a felony assault with a . . ." He consulted the file. ". . . piece of luggage, the injured parties aren't pressing charges. We'll be with you in a bit to process the paperwork, and then you'll be free to leave." The officer walked away, and Julia glanced at the man beside her.

"*Why* are you smiling?" she wanted to know.

"That guy . . . well, everyone really, they think that you and I are . . . well, I know it's not true, but I'm flattered that they would think it could be."

*What's that supposed to mean?* Julia wondered. She looked around for photographers or reporters, but everyone else in the room was busy with the troubles of their own lives—no one seemed to be paying attention to hers. No one except Lance.

Julia studied him, then asked, "That was a compliment, wasn't it?"

"Not a compliment," Lance said. "Just a statement of fact."

Julia put her hands under her thighs and swung her legs like she and Caroline used to do when they were girls. She felt little again, not young but small, sitting on this very tall, very uncomfortable bench. She wondered if this was how it felt to get sent to the principal's office, to wait side by side with the eighth-grade bully. But Lance wasn't a bully. And this whole thing wasn't his fault. It was time to tell him so.

"It's not your fault," she said. "I know that. I believe you."

"Thank you," he said simply, taking the apology with grace.

"And your people were not the only ones to get carried away. They *started* it," she said, emphasizing the point. "But my editor, well, my ex-editor, he fell for it, too."

"I'm sorry," Lance said, sounding sincere.

"That's okay," Julia said, calling on her emotional reserves. "I have an early flight. I'm going back to the people I love. I'm leaving, and this will all be over."

"Great."

"Six thirty this morning, and I'm out of here," she stated flatly.

"Six thirty? Your flight's at six thirty, or you're leaving for the airport at six thirty?" Lance glanced at the clock on the wall behind her. "Because it's four fifteen in the morning right now."

Julia turned to study the clock herself. "It can't be!"

"It is." He raised his eyebrows in mock reverence. "Welcome to the criminal justice system."

"I'm not going to make it," Julia exclaimed, wilting with the realization. "It's her fifth birthday, and I'm not going to make it."

They sat in silence for a few moments. Then Lance turned to her. "What if I was to make sure you made that flight? What would that be worth?"

Julia leaned her head against the notice-covered bulletin

board. She heard paper crinkle and felt a thumbtack jab into her skull, but she was far too exhausted to care. "If I made it to the airport with all of my belongings in time to catch a six thirty A.M. flight?"

"Yeah," he said.

"If you could do that, you could name your price. But since—"

"I need to make a call," Lance said to a passing guard. A moment later, he was gone, leaving Julia on that hard bench alone.

♣

Forty minutes later, Lance appeared at Julia's elbow. "Come on," he said, holding her coat. "Let's sign the forms and go."

"What? We're ready?"

"Well, I don't know about you, but I am."

The frigid March air hit Julia like a fist as they exited the station, and she recoiled, leaning into Lance. To her surprise, in spite of the hour, a cab was idling on the street at the bottom of the steep stairs. As they reached the sidewalk, the back door of the cab opened and a young man got out. Lance nodded at him and asked, "Everything set?"

"It's all in there," the young man responded. "I signed her out of her room, too."

"Okay." Lance moved to shake hands with his friend. "I owe you."

"Damn right you do."

"Will someone please tell me what's going on here?" Julia asked.

"Oh, sorry." The young man stepped forward and held his hand out for Julia to shake, which she did. "How ya doing?"

"Julia James"—Lance put his arm around her—"I'd like you to meet Tom Ford, a friend of mine." Lance ran his free hand through his hair, a gesture that almost succeeded in muffling his voice when he added, "Tom's also a bellman at the Ritz."

"Oh," Julia said, allowing a lot of pieces to fall into the puzzle.

"Tom and I are members of New York's thespian underground," Lance explained. "There's not a hotel we can't get into, a restaurant we can't eat at, or a Gap where we can't get an employee discount. We're very powerful. Don't mess with us," he joked.

Tom raised his eyebrow in a "yep, I'm guilty" gesture. Julia looked at her carry-on bags lying in the backseat of the cab and forgot about invasion of privacy and hotel security, serenely grateful that Tom had chosen to abuse his power for a good cause.

"Come on." Lance pushed her toward the running taxi. "We've got a plane to catch." With a wave back at Tom, he said, "Thanks, man. Good luck in LA."

Julia was almost in the cab when she registered the "we."

"We? What do you mean 'We've got a plane to catch'?"

Through the diluted light of a streetlamp, Lance surveyed the exhausted woman who was halfway into the cab with one foot on the back floorboard and one hand on the top of the car. There were a couple of ways he could force her into the car from that position, none of which he would try in front of a police station.

He held out his hands. "Julia, I'm a bartender. I work nights and, as you can tell, I didn't show up tonight, so I'm probably fired. I don't have an agent, not one that I'm proud of anyway. I'm not scheduled for any auditions. And yet my picture is on every newsstand in America. You don't know me, but you have to believe me when I say that I am a good actor and I don't want to get ahead this way. Believe it or not, I'm an honorable guy. But honorable or not, I've still got to make rent. If I stay here, I'm gonna stumble, and then you're going to go down with me. I don't want to do that. Remove the temptation, please. Just get me away from this town for a while. Let's regroup. Let's put our heads together. Let's do it in Tulsa."

She shifted. He saw her start to budge. She shifted again, and he wished she'd just get in the stupid cab. He wasn't wearing a heavy coat, and it was freezing out. He tried one more piece of truth. "You're here with me, or you're there with me. It's your call, but the clock is ticking. And you said I could name my price."

She slid into the backseat and said, "Let's go."

# Chapter Seven

> **WAY #47: Get out of town.**
> If there's a place you've always wanted to see—go there. If
> there's an adventure you've always wanted to experience—do
> it. Traveling isn't just for couples anymore.
>
> —from *101 Ways to Cheat at Solitaire*

Julia hated to call so early, but the flight was boarding soon and she didn't know when she'd get another chance. Caroline's greeting was groggy but to the point.

"How's it going, slugger?"

"You heard?" Julia asked, cringing.

"Oh, I *saw*. There was news footage. What were you thinking—"

"Please, C, please don't start. I've been sitting in a police station hallway all night. So, please, if we can do this conversation later, I would really appreciate it."

"Sure," her sister said. "We'll do it when you get home."

"Well . . . see . . ." *Just spit it out, Julia,* she told herself. "I won't be alone."

"I *knew* it!" Caroline cried. "As soon as I saw that picture, I just knew in my gut! He looks just like—"

"Caroline!" Julia cut her off.

"What? Can't I say it? Doesn't he know he's the spitting image of—"

"Caroline, cut it out. We're not 'together' together. Making the flight was kind of iffy, and there was a price attached. I've got to take him with me. But it's okay. I can keep an eye on him this way, keep things from escalating. So, please, just brief the troops."

"Whatever you say," Caroline said. "Whatever you say," she repeated, not trying to disguise her skepticism.

Julia looked across the terminal at the man waiting for her by the glass and told herself that everything was for the best. Then Lance yawned and stretched, and she saw half the women in the airport drop their purses and their jaws at the sight of him. *Oh, well,* she thought, *that which does not kill us makes us stronger.* She said good-bye to her sister and snapped her phone shut.

Lance took this as his cue to make a call himself.

"Everything okay?" he asked as he walked past.

She cut her eyes up at him and said, "Fine."

He slid a quarter into a pay phone and dialed a familiar number. He told the operator that the call would be collect, something he no longer felt guilty about. The guilt he did have came from calling at what was essentially the middle of the night in

California. But knowing his mother and her chronic insomnia, Lance half suspected she might be repotting petunias or vacuuming the oven instead of in the middle of a dream. Whatever the case, he was sure she'd want to know what was going on.

"They're not true," he said instead of hello as soon as he heard his mother's voice.

"Well, I knew that," she said, her voice utterly awake, her response to the point. Lance realized then how much he'd missed his mother's shorthand. With other people, things needed to be explained, sentences needed to be finished. When he was talking to the woman who'd raised him, all adjectives and most verbs became virtually useless.

"So," she said, "are you going to tell me what's going on?"

"Do you want me to?"

"Not really. As long as you're okay."

"I am. I'm good."

"Sweetheart," she started, and he knew very well where that sentence was going to end up.

"Don't, Mom. Please."

"But he's your father," she pleaded. "He'd want to—"

"You didn't need his help when you were raising me. I don't need it now."

"Okay," she said, backing down. "You're okay?" she asked again.

"Yeah," he said. "I'm okay. Look, I'm going to drop off the radar for a little while. Don't worry if you don't hear from me for a day or two." From the corner of his eye, he saw a newsstand full of tabloids. "And if you read anything about me," he went on, "don't believe it."

The line was silent for a long time, and Lance wondered if the call had been disconnected. Then he heard his mother say, "This sounds like something—"

"Dad's *not* a factor in this."

"You'll call if you need anything?" she asked him.

"Of course," he said and told her good-bye.

♥

Julia was in first class; Lance was stuck in coach. Well, not really stuck. She'd put him there under the guise of not wanting to draw attention to themselves by traveling together, and he'd bought it. Or he didn't care. Whatever the case, she stretched out in the leather seat, ate her warm croissant, and got ready to sleep until they had to change planes in Dallas. Without delays, they'd touch down in Tulsa at one and be at her sister's in plenty of time for Cassie's three-o'clock party.

Her heavy eyelids had just begun to drop when she heard, "Excuse me," and opened one eye to see a flight attendant hovering overhead. "I'm sorry to bother you, Miss James. It's just that I'm such a huge fan. The airline usually frowns on this sort of thing," the young woman said as she reached into the pocket of her smock, "but if you could . . ." She held a copy of *101 Ways to Cheat at Solitaire* and a pen toward Julia.

*An autograph,* Julia thought, feeling as if the last few days had been a dream and she was just flying out of New York, not fleeing from it. Her book was in her hands; a woman who appreciated her message stood before her. *This is who I am,* Julia thought. *This is what I do.* Her confidence soared. Two lines inside the cover. A signature. A smile.

She took the book, opened to the front page, and saw that someone had beaten her to it.

> *To Marci,*
> *All the best,*
> *Lance Collins*

When the passengers back in coach were finally allowed to deplane, Lance followed the masses through the airport.

Julia was nowhere to be seen. The staff at the Ritz had shipped the bulk of her toy purchases home for her, but she still had suitcases and other bags. Lance knew she might have ditched *him,* but she wasn't going home without her luggage. He stood on his tiptoes and scanned the baggage-claim area when a noise flew past his ear like a gnat.

"Pssst. Pssst."

*Where was that coming from?*

"Behind the ficus."

He started to pivot.

"Don't turn around!"

Lance faced forward, away from rustling of fake ferns and plastic trees that came from an exhibit designed to encourage visitors to check out the Tulsa Zoo while they were in town.

Among the stuffed monkeys and rubber snakes, Julia was hiding with her scarf wrapped around her head.

"Exactly what are you doing?" Lance wanted to know.

"I am waiting for you to claim our bags. Then you and I are leaving without anyone knowing we're here."

"Okay," Lance said, placating her, as he realized that not every crazy person in the world lived in Manhattan.

Julia's suitcases tumbled onto the circular belt, followed by his own bag. He claimed them, and once the luggage was in hand, he proceeded directly out the glass doors and into one of the most beautiful spring days he had ever seen. When they'd left New York, it had been dreary and twenty-five degrees. But in Tulsa, the sun was out and the temperature must have been at least sixty-five. He stood, soaking up the vitamin D until Julia emerged from the airport, removing the scarf, freeing her hair to billow in the Oklahoma wind. Strands blew across her face, and he wanted to brush them away, but before he could say or do a thing, he heard a raspy voice behind him.

"He's tall," the woman said. "That's good, Jules. We like tall."

Lance turned to see a woman who was in every way the opposite of her voice: small and feminine, with olive skin and refined features.

"I'm Nina." The tiny, raspy little woman extended her hand. "I'm her best friend."

"I'm Lance."

"I know," Nina squealed. "You're her boyfriend!"

# Chapter Eight

WAY #54: It's better to be single and happy than
married and miserable.
One of the biggest challenges you'll face is the "Why haven't
you been married?" phenomenon. Dealing with this is simple:
Ignore it. And pity the culture that looks more favorably on
those who have bad marriages than those who choose to remain single.

—from *101 Ways to Cheat at Solitaire*

Ten minutes later, they were flying down the highway in
Nina's vintage VW. She had pushed aside piles of fab-
ric samples and magazines to make room for Lance in
the backseat. "It's a project," Nina had explained. What kind
of project, Lance certainly wasn't going to ask, because he
wanted Nina to stay as focused on the road as possible. Maybe
it was the way his six-two body had been folded into the tiny
car, but when they began to swerve between semis, he knew

for a fact that he might die there, in the back of a bug, surrounded by pieces of velvet.

"Ro-Ro's coming," Nina said casually.

Julia wheeled around in the front seat and nearly kicked the
car out of gear.

"No!" she yelled.

"Yes," Nina snapped back.

"Ro-Ro doesn't come to birthday parties," Julia argued.
"Ro-Ro sends recycled cards and dingy five-dollar bills."

"Who's Ro-Ro?" Lance asked from the backseat.

Julia buried her head in her palm then bolted upright
again and exclaimed, "Ro-Ro doesn't come to birthday parties!"

"Well, she's coming to this one," Nina said with resolve.

"She knows, doesn't she?"

"That's my bet."

"Who's Ro-Ro?" Lance asked again, but the women had
evidently forgotten he existed.

"But, how does she know? Mom and Dad wouldn't tell her,
and they're the only people who ever call her. She's got her
maids scared half to death. She doesn't even own a television."

"True," Nina said with raised eyebrows. "But the Georgias do."

"Oh." Julia slumped in the seat again and moaned, "The
Georgias."

"You are a hot topic on the Tulsa bridge circuit today!"

Nina laughed. "I bet they crash the party just to get a look at him." She gestured to Lance in the backseat.

"Ro-Ro's coming," Julia said with dread. "And she's bringing the Georgias."

Nina joyfully added, "That's right!"

Lance leaned between the seats and yelled, "WHO IS RO-RO?"

Julia waved dismissively at Nina and said, "Tell him."

Nina glanced at Lance in the rearview mirror. "Ro-Ro is Julia's aunt."

"*Great* aunt," Julia corrected.

"Right," Nina said, then carried on as if this was the beginning of her all-time favorite story. "She's Rosemary Crane Willis Fitzgerald, and in this town, she's famous."

"You call her Ro-Ro?" Lance asked, thinking he was catching on.

"Oh, heavens no," Nina said. "Not to her face. To her face, family calls her Aunt Rosemary, and vagrants like you and I call her Mrs. Willis."

"Why Willis?" Lance asked. "Why not one of the other ones?"

"Willis was the husband she liked best," Nina answered patiently.

"Hated least," Julia corrected.

"Whatever," Nina said. "She's a piece of work. Married four times. Widowed four times. Each husband richer than the one who came before him. Plus, she's tighter than a submarine and older than the hills."

"Married four times?" Lance questioned. "You only gave three last names."

"Two of the husbands were brothers," Julia clarified.

"She never leaves her house unless she's on the warpath about something." Nina reached over and patted Julia's thigh. "But she's coming today."

Julia moaned, and Lance raised his eyebrows.

"And then," Nina stated with flair, "we have the Georgias—also known as Georgia Abernathy, Georgia Burke, and Evelyn Wesley, who was Miss Georgia in 1954. They all live in Ro-Ro's building and follow her around like little blue-haired disciples, especially Miss Georgia A. and Miss Georgia B. I think Miss Georgia '54 would like to lead her own gang, but as long as Ro-Ro's living there, no ex–beauty queen has got a prayer of forming any kind of splinter group."

"Sounds like 90210, the golden years," Lance joked.

"Exactly," Nina said, nodding her approval.

Lance began to wonder what he'd gotten himself into.

"Don't worry," Nina reassured him. "You'll do great!"

Julia cringed and sank a little deeper into the seat.

◆

When they stopped for gas, Lance insisted on getting out and pumping. Nina insisted on letting him.

"He is the biggest problem my career has ever faced, and

instead of leaving him in New York"—Julia gestured to where Lance stood beside the car—"I let him follow me home," she exclaimed, rolling her eyes skyward, finishing a five-minute monologue on "the Lance Situation." She looked to Nina for sympathy, but all she saw was her best friend's outstretched hand. "I'm not wearing the ring, or did you notice?"

"I did notice, and I'm proud," Julia said, and gave herself a mental slap for not being more sensitive. But it was hard not to grow immune to the drama of Nina's love life, especially after watching her marry and divorce the same man twice.

"Jason's totally moved out, and we've filed the papers. So . . ." There was a drumroll in her voice. "In eight weeks, I'll be a single gal!" she finished with a big *ta-da*!

Nina must have confused Julia's silence for self-pity because she said, "Come on, Jules, let's keep things in perspective here. You meet a hot guy. Great. Worse ways to spend a day. People think you've got feelings for the hot guy. Hardly a national crisis. Besides"—she stopped and gestured to Lance, who stood dutifully beside the car—"he pumps the gas. I don't even remember the last time I didn't have to pump my own gas."

Both women stared at him out the window.

When Lance took the squeegee and began to clean the windshield, Nina gripped the steering wheel and moaned, "Oh, have mercy."

♠

"Which house is it again?" Nina asked as they pulled into a housing addition a half mile off the highway. Lance looked around and understood why she was confused. The subdivision was like a maze, each structure nearly identical to the one that stood beside it, all of them in the last stages of completion, each one reeking of decay as muddy, un-sodded yards oozed into piles of shingles and scrap lumber.

"What is going on here?" Lance asked.

"Contractor went bankrupt," Nina told him. "There are only three or four houses in the whole subdivision that are done. Everything else is in limbo. No one can finish them until the courts straighten it out."

"What a mess," he muttered.

"This is the road," Julia said, guiding Nina onto a snakelike lane that resembled every other road in the monster development. They eased their way through the half-finished carnage of dream homes until they made another twist and saw one house that had daffodils dotting the flowerbeds and an abandoned tricycle standing sentry in the yard. Orange and white helium-filled balloons were tied to the mailbox and drifted in the breeze, but there wasn't another car in sight.

"Good," Nina said as she pulled the VW up the slight incline of the garage slab and shifted into park. "We're early."

# Chapter Nine

*here are some things the world should be spared, and the sight of a tax attorney in a Hello Kitty party hat is one of them,* Julia thought as she stood in the doorway of her sister's house and examined her brother-in-law, Steve. Then she recognized the strange feeling in her stomach: *relief.* Maybe she was simply glad that Steve had placed his family over his firm for at least a few hours that weekend, but deep down, Julia realized the feeling was probably due to the fact that of all the people she could count on not to notice the

Lance debacle and not to care, her brother-in-law was at the top of the list.

"Julia, welcome back," Steve said, as if ushering her into his office.

"Like the hat," Nina said as she followed Julia inside.

"Hi there," Lance said, and held out his hand. "I'm Lance."

"Welcome, Lance," Steve said, shaking his hand. "Come on in."

In the grand foyer, their footsteps echoed on the marble floor, despite the gorgeous rugs and wall hangings that Nina had sold to Caroline at cost, earning her a place in Steve's penny-pinching heart forever. A staircase curved to the second story and the formal living room stretched out beneath a cathedral ceiling, and Julia had to wonder for the millionth time how her sister and brother-in-law had wound up here. It looked like a page from a magazine, and it had been Julia's experience that only two-dimensional people live in such two-dimensional rooms. But the chandelier kept blazing, and all six thousand square feet of it kept gathering dust—despite Caroline's constant efforts otherwise.

Steve led the way through a formal dining room that Julia had never seen anyone use. They were about to enter the kitchen when her sister screamed, "I'm going to kill her!"

"Now, Caroline, sweetheart, you shouldn't harbor darkness in your heart."

*Great, Mom's here,* Julia thought. But Caroline was having none of their mother's goodness and wisdom.

"Mom, you misunderstood. I didn't say I hated her, I said I was going to kill her."

Steve, Julia, Nina, and Lance exchanged glances as Caroline shrieked, "That old bat is trying to ruin my daughter's party!"

Nina leaned close to Julia and whispered, "Ro-Ro?"

"I don't think so," Julia whispered back. A loud crash echoed through the house, and Steve bolted toward the noise, muttering, "That sounded expensive!" The rest of them hurried along behind him.

"That is our backyard!" Caroline was saying as they all entered the kitchen. "Three different surveyors were here, and they all agreed on the property line. So help me, if she pulls up one more stake, I'm going to stick it up her . . ."

Caroline stopped short at the newcomers' arrival. Then everyone seemed to stare at Lance, who looked wrinkled and worn. Julia knew how exhausted she was, and thought that he must be about to collapse, too; he certainly looked like it.

"Julia, welcome back," her mother said at last. "Aren't you going to introduce your friend?"

*Friend.* Not sweetheart or parasite or stalker. *Friend.* She could handle that.

"Lance Collins, this is my mother, Madelyn, and my sister, Caroline. You met Steve and Nina. Everyone, you probably know about Lance."

The grins on the women's faces said that yes, they knew all about Lance. Steve's vacant expression said that he was wondering what would happen to the 248b deduction when Congress met next session. For the first time ever, Julia wished the rest of her family was more like Steve.

"Sweetheart," Steve said to Caroline. "Did I hear something break?"

"Oh, Steve, I'm fine," Caroline told him.

"But what broke?" he persisted.

"It was a pickle jar, Steve," Madelyn said, obviously understanding what her son-in-law was getting at. "And don't worry, it was empty. No precious pickles went to waste."

Steve seemed to visibly relax.

"Lance, won't you come over here and sit down?" Madelyn gestured to one of the barstools surrounding Caroline's granite-covered island. "You must be exhausted. Did you have a nice trip?"

"He had a fine trip, Mother," Julia said, but Madelyn cut her a look that mothers never lose, no matter how many years removed from the womb their children are.

"I was talking to Lance, Julia Marie. I was speaking to your guest."

"Hey, don't jump on me. Caroline's the one premeditating murder," Julia said, quietly relieved that there was a major crisis on the table, something—anything—to take the focus off her and the stray that she'd brought home.

Caroline sighed and screamed into a dishrag. When she came up for air, she explained: "Crazy Myrtle is about to be the death of me."

"Caroline," Madelyn interceded, "don't you think you're being a little harsh?"

"She goes through our trash," Caroline said with the finality of someone laying down a trump card.

"No way does she actually do that." Nina laughed.

"Oh yes she does," Caroline said defiantly. "She goes out there in her bathrobe before the garbage men come. She'll dig around, and if she finds something she likes, she'll take it." Before anyone could protest this bold revelation, Caroline raised her right hand and said, "I swear."

"Well, what do you do about it?" Nina asked.

"The first time we ignored it, but after a month, Steve went over there, and the crazy bat laughed and slammed the door in his face." Caroline took a bottle of kitchen cleaner and sprayed her already spotless counter, then picked up the rag and began scrubbing with a vengeance.

"Now"—Caroline sighed—"she's complaining about the property line. She's probably out there pulling up markers even as we speak. Forty-seven empty houses in this place, and the only other occupied one is next to us. Is it a nice young family with kids the same age as ours? No. It's the crazy mother of the crazy contractor who went bankrupt and is now trying to drive me completely crazy." She turned to her husband. "I swear, if she so much as crosses a toe over our property line during Cassie's party, I'll—"

"Call the police!" Steve supplied.

"No, Steve, our daughter is not going to be the only

child in preschool to have the cops bust up her birthday party."

Madelyn tossed her hands into the air. "Lance, don't look at us," she said. "Turn away. This is not a proud moment for the James family. I am so ashamed." She turned and went through the French doors and out onto the patio.

Julia watched her mother leave, and then she wondered where her normally docile sister had gone. Caroline must have read Julia's mind, because she held her hands out to her side and said, "Myrtle makes me crazy."

"I hope my being here didn't embarrass your mother too much," Lance said.

"Don't worry about it. There's dip out there. That's all she really needs," Caroline said and threw the rag into the sink.

"Where are the munchkins?" Julia asked, looking around for her niece and nephew.

"Oh, no," Caroline said. "You need a shower and a nap first. Trust me." She pushed Julia toward the stairs. "Steve, get Nina's keys and bring Julia's bags in. Lance's, too. They've got to clean up. And then I want you to go get the spraypaint in the garage and mark the ground between the stakes so that we'll know where the line is when the fence people show up."

"But, honey—" Steve started. One look at Caroline changed his tune to "Yes, dear," and the Hello Kitty hat was out the door.

♣

"There you are, sleepyhead," Julia's father said.

"Hi Daddy," Julia said, and leaned down to kiss the top of

his head. After a long shower and a quick nap, the only thing she needed to feel completely renewed was the sight of her father sitting in the formal living room, reading the newspaper, his bifocals low on his nose.

"It's good to see you, honey."

"You, too," she said, taking a seat on the edge of the table in front of him.

He folded his paper and said, "You almost missed the party."

Julia grinned. "Isn't that what you're doing?"

He smiled and adjusted his grip on the paper and said, "If I stay quiet enough, they'll forget about me, and I might just get it done."

She watched her father shift in the tasteful furniture, and she could tell that even here, in his youngest daughter's enormous house, he felt fenced in. Bill James was a man for whom six thousand square feet would never be enough room. And as Julia sat there, studying him, she realized that the older she got, the more she became her father's daughter.

"Have we had any rain?" she asked him.

He nodded his head and said, "Enough."

"How are we for hay?"

"Good shape. Good shape. I think we're going to get that bull bought."

"That's great," she said, feigning normalcy, but her breaking throat betrayed her. "Daddy . . ."

"It's okay, sweetie," he said. His big hands fell over both of hers, the universal father signal for *you're still my little girl.* "It's gonna be okay," he told her. "Now, go, enjoy the party."

She hugged him, then moved toward the noise.

"But I'd watch out for Ro-Ro," he called after her.

Through the French doors of the family room, Julia saw that Cassie and her friends were engaged in a fiery game of duck-duck-goose on the back lawn. Ro-Ro was settled on a wicker chair, with Steve waiting dutifully at her side. A number of parents stood around, playing referee. But Julia didn't follow the action; she followed the voices.

"I like him," Nina said as Julia neared the kitchen. "He laughs when he's supposed to, and he wears good shoes. You can tell a lot about a man by his shoes."

"I don't think it matters what we think. Julia doesn't like him," Caroline stated flatly.

"How can you tell?" Nina asked.

"Because men make Julia uncomfortable."

"Caroline, I don't think you're being fair to your sister," her mother replied.

"I love her, Mother. Aside from my own children, I love her more than anybody in the world, but my sister is—"

"Listening to every word you say." Looks of remorse passed over the three faces as they stared at Julia in the doorway. "Caroline, you're right, I'm not interested in him. And Mother, thank you for defending my honor. That seems to be needed a lot lately," Julia said, walking toward them.

"Honey," her mother asked, "how are you feeling?"

"The last two days haven't been a dream, have they?"

Nina shook her head. "Nope."

Julia sighed. "Where is he?" she asked.

"With the kids. He's doing magic tricks. He's really good," Caroline added, as if that would make the situation better.

"I know. He's already made my dignity disappear." Julia climbed onto one of the barstools and picked up a sugar cookie in the shape of a balloon.

"Okay, crew." Nina slapped her hands together. "This is the brain trust. It's time to formulate a plan. I say we call Candon and set up—"

"Candon's history," Julia said. "He saw the sales numbers and got greedy. I am officially finished with Candon."

"Well, then we'll get Harvey—" Caroline started.

"Harvey had a heart attack."

"Oh my," Madelyn exclaimed. "Have you sent flowers?"

"No, Mom, I've been busy having a fictitious affair."

"Well, that's no reason not to send flowers," Madelyn said, amazed.

*No, but the fact that I gave him the heart attack might be,* Julia thought.

"Julia," Caroline said, "what are you going to *do*?"

"Maybe a houseplant?" Madelyn interjected.

"I don't know, Caroline," Julia snapped, ignoring her mother and growing irritated with her sister. She didn't have an answer. She didn't have a clue. "I'm going to sleep in my own bed tonight. I'm going to spend time with the kids. I'm going to wrap my mind around this and come up with something."

"Cut flowers die," Madelyn afforded, as if clicking through the "in case of death or hospitalization" registry in her head. "I don't think that's the right message, you know, under the *circumstances,*" she whispered, as if Harvey could hear her and she didn't want to be caught speaking ill of the almost-dead.

It was only then that Julia realized how alone she was in this. Anyone in that house would have lain down in front of a train if she'd asked them, but for her future in publishing, their efforts would be just as pointless. There was one thing, however, that they could do.

"So, Sis, which room did you put Lance in?"

"No." Caroline shook her head, seeing where her sister was heading.

"Come on, his stuff is already upstairs!"

"He's a stranger. He's not sleeping under my roof."

"Would you rather he sleep under mine?" Julia asked. "You've got *Steve*. You'll be *safe*."

"Oh, yeah," Nina interjected, " 'cause when I think *bodyguard,* I always think *Steve*."

"Hey," Caroline snapped.

"Nina." Julia turned to her best friend. "Can't he stay with you?"

Nina seemed to ponder this. "Tempting, but no. I am this close"—she held her thumb and forefinger inches apart from each other—"to having my divorce finalized. If Jason thought

I was living with another man, who knows what hell he'd raise. Besides, you're the one who brought Lance home; now you're going to have to *feed* him and *water* him and take him out when he needs to go."

"Mom?" Julia tried her last option.

"No," Madelyn said. "Julia, Nina's right."

"I am?" Nina said, not really believing it.

Madelyn finished: "This is your responsibility."

# Chapter Ten

> **WAY #82: Honor your ancestors.**
> Families are rich in history. As you seek to make sense of your own life, go back a few generations and learn about the people who went before you. Sift through the years, and you may find answers in their ashes.
>
> —from *101 Ways to Cheat at Solitaire*

The little raisin of a woman who summoned Lance from across the party couldn't have weighed more than a hundred pounds, Lance decided, not counting the diamonds. Nina had told him that Ro-Ro's first husband had owned a diamond mine in South Africa, so naturally, she'd started off with a big ring. As Lance studied her tiny hands, he could see how hard it must have been for husbands two through four to keep up. What Lance couldn't surmise was whether Ro-Ro was deeply connected to the dead loves of her life and wore their rings to remember them, or if she kept the jewels on her at all times simply because she needed the attention and didn't trust the help.

"You must be Julia's fella," she said, once he had settled beside her.

"Actually, ma'am, it's a little more—"

"Don't contradict me, young man."

"Yes, ma'am."

She looked him up and down as if she was thinking about buying him at auction. "What is your profession?" she asked.

"I'm an actor."

She grunted in a way that left Lance unsure of her meaning. "*I* was an actress," she said, emphasis on the *I*, as if to infer that he was a mere impostor.

"Stage or screen?" he asked, trying to sound impressed.

Ro-Ro cut her tiny eyes toward him, insulted. "Stage, of course."

"Of course," Lance hurried to agree. "What were you in?"

Ro-Ro seemed to consider her answer very carefully before saying, "I only lived in New York for a short time before my Wally came for me and I married him. But I would have been great! They no doubt still say what a great loss it was to the theater when I married and gave up what would have been a monumental career."

Lance struggled for a response but was saved when a series of shadows appeared suddenly at his side. He looked up at a line of rayon suits and matching handbags, blue hair and knowing grins, and he could only assume that the Georgias had arrived.

"Rosemary, darling, isn't this a happy day?" the smallest of the women squealed as she leaned down and gave Ro-Ro a weak hug.

"Georgia," Ro-Ro said with a nod, barely acknowledging her subordinate.

"And you must be the young man we've all heard so much about. How do you do? I'm Georgia Abernathy. I'm a great friend of the family."

Lance stood and shook her frail hand. "Lance Collins, ma'am. Nice to meet you."

All the Georgias looked at one another and giggled. Lance guessed that he had just passed their initial test. Georgia Abernathy continued to speak, introducing Georgia Burke and Miss Georgia '54, even though Lance could have easily saved her the trouble. Between Georgia B. and Evelyn Wesley, there was very little doubt which one was the former beauty queen. The former Miss Georgia could have given women half her age a run for their money, whereas Georgia B. had probably never turned many heads, even in her youth. While Evelyn Wesley had a waiflike presence that denoted her as a woman who had probably never been larger than a size six, Georgia Burke had the large bones and wide hips of a woman who'd been born to work and breed. But what Georgia B. lacked in traditional beauty, she made up for in spirit, Lance could see. When she hugged him and said, "It's so *nice* to meet you," Lance felt that she genuinely meant it.

"Oh, Rosemary," Miss Georgia said to Ro-Ro, "I hope you

were telling Lance about the benefit tomorrow night." She laid one of her perfectly manicured hands on his arm, "You and Julia simply must come with Rosemary. It's going to be the event of the year."

"Evelyn," Ro-Ro cut in, "to you, they are all the event of the year."

"Well," Miss Georgia carried on, "it certainly is the event of the *spring*. If you've never seen Sycamore Hills in the spring, it's worth coming just for that. Oh, the dogwoods and the Easter lilies and the . . . well, it's simply gorgeous! I do hope you'll be able to come." She smiled, and Lance guessed that thousands of men before him had probably had a hard time saying no to Evelyn Wesley.

But Ro-Ro didn't let him answer. "I have no tolerance for those ridiculous affairs," she said. "I will not go. No doubt my family will have no interest in going."

"Rosemary, if you hate events like this, why did you buy a table?" Miss Georgia challenged.

"People expect a woman of my standing to contribute, so I contribute."

Georgia A. stepped in. "You can't have an empty table."

Georgia B. agreed. "It would look awkward. I'll talk to the organizers—have them take your table down."

"No," Ro-Ro snapped, then seemed to consider her options. "Although I loathe those functions, I concede they have worth." She looked at Lance as if seeing whether or not he would meet some secret set of standards. Then she straightened her back and folded her hands in her lap, assumed the posture of a queen handing down a decree, and said, "My nieces will attend on my behalf. It's time for them to learn to do their part."

"Ooh!" Miss Georgia squealed. "We are going to have a wonderful time!"

♥

"So, what do we have planned for tomorrow night?" Lance asked when he found Julia, Nina, and Caroline in the kitchen. "Because I was talking to Ro-Ro—"

Caroline cut him off. "I'm sorry about that. I told Steve to keep her busy." She scanned the party for her husband. "Steve," she yelled out the window when she saw him. "Isn't there someone you're supposed to be watching?" And in a flash, Steve bolted toward Ro-Ro and the Georgias on the far side of the yard. Caroline turned her attention back to Lance. "Again, I'm sorry about that," she said.

"That's okay. I kind of liked her," Lance said, and Julia choked on her Diet Coke.

Caroline snickered. "Did you just say you kind of like Ro-Ro?"

"She's got spunk," Lance said.

"Well, that's one way of putting it," Julia said.

"Kind of like someone else I know."

"Whatever," Julia said, dismissing him.

"Anyway, I was talking with her when the Georgias came and, well, one thing led to another, and now I think we all have to go to a party tomorrow night at some place called Sycamore Hills." Lance waited for the blast of steam Julia might let off, but nothing happened.

Julia shrugged. "Oh, one of those? Don't worry, we don't have to go."

"But Ro-Ro bought a table and—"

"Ro-Ro's always buying tables for whatever cause her little group is supporting that week. She never goes. We never go. Trust me, it's nothing."

"Jules, you have to go, and you have to take me!" Nina cried. "I have it on good authority that Sycamore Hills just spent a hundred grand on curtains for the ballroom. I've got to see them. I want to *feel* them. Please! Can you imagine the business I could drum up in that place? Those people are all gazillionaires, and I bet none of them have hired a decorator since Nixon resigned!"

"What's the cause?" Caroline asked Lance.

"It is a benefit for the Junior Symphony," he told her.

"Great!" Nina exclaimed. "Underprivileged cellists. I can get behind that."

Caroline spoke softly near her sister's ear. "Jules, no one at Sycamore Hills is going to talk to the press, if that's what you're worried about. Not even the staff. Those people are old-school. The CIA can learn secret-keeping tips from the Sycamore Hills crowd, believe me."

"C'mon Jules," Nina said, a wicked smile spreading across her face. "You can go to a big, flashy, expensive party and help out your *best friend*, or you could stay home. Alone. With Lance."

Julia threw back her shoulders and said, "I support the symphony."

◆

"Cassie, what do you say?" Caroline prompted, but even Julia didn't know how to respond to the Georgias' present.

"Thank you?" Cassie tried, but one look at the child's face said that an antique porcelain doll with an accompanying semiprecious tiara hadn't been on Cassie's wish list.

"The tiara will fit you, too, dear," Miss Georgia said, removing it from the doll's head and placing it on Cassie's. "Oh," Miss Georgia sighed. "There she is . . . our Miss Cassie."

"Here, sweetie," Caroline said, grabbing the fragile doll from Cassie's grasp, no doubt already calculating how many pieces it would shatter into with even a short drop onto the hard floor. "That was very nice, ladies. Very . . ." Caroline struggled for words, "generous."

The Georgias looked at one another, proud of themselves. Ro-Ro scowled in the corner, her card and five-dollar bill having been sufficiently outdone.

"This is the first time I've been to your home, Caroline," Ro-Ro said, her voice bouncing off the tile floor and echoing beneath the cathedral ceiling. *Just what we need,* Julia mused, *Ro-Ro in stereo.* "Exactly how large *is* it?" Her gaze scanned the formal living room, settling on the second-story balcony.

Caroline's voice was shaky as she answered: "A little over five thousand seven hundred."

"It's too large," Ro-Ro snapped quickly. "*My* apartment is one thousand square feet. That's a *nice* size. That's the size of home you should live in."

"Rosemary," Madelyn was quick to defend her baby girl. "Caroline has two small children. She and Steve need a large house."

"Nonsense. This house is too large. You should sell it, but of course, there aren't many people foolish enough to buy it. Pity you didn't ask me. I could have saved you a lot of time and expense."

Instead of responding, Caroline bolted toward the kitchen. "It's time for cake!"

Undaunted, Ro-Ro carried on. "When Uncle Gregory and I lived in Lisbon, we had a house that was nearly ten thousand square feet."

"But that's twice as big as this house!" Madelyn exclaimed. "You didn't think *that* was excessive?"

"That was Portugal," Ro-Ro bit back. "Everyone who's anyone has a large home in Portugal. In Tulsa, I have a one-thousand-square-foot apartment." She didn't say that therefore, everyone who's anyone in Tulsa has a one thousand-square-foot apartment. That part was implied.

"Uncle Sherman had a home in Costa Rica," Ro-Ro went on. "You girls don't remember Uncle Sherman, of course," Ro-Ro said. Julia thought, *That would be hard, considering he died in 1922.* "He had a gold mine there. He always said that Heaven would look like Costa Rica. I guess he'll never know."

They all stared at one another, so Ro-Ro added, "Uncle Sherman was a terrible man."

"You've led a fascinating life, Aunt Rosemary," Julia said, and fought the urge to add, *Now shut up about it.*

"Yes, I have. It's a shame I'll be dead soon and will no longer be able to share my experiences."

They all nodded in agreement, not sure whether she was fishing for the "Oh, you're still a young woman, Aunt Rosemary" speech or the "Oh, you're the only bright spot in our lives, Aunt Rosemary" speech. Whatever the case, the James family had learned years before that the safest thing to do was nod.

"That settles it," the old woman shouted with spunk. "I will stay here tonight, and tomorrow morning, Caroline will help me write my memoirs."

A crash came from the doorway. Julia wheeled around to see Caroline standing there, her arms outstretched but empty; the birthday cake she had spent six hours baking and decorating from scratch lay at her feet in a heap of frosting and smoke, as five crooked candles burned in the rubble. Caroline stood in the mouth of the massive room, gasping, not even noticing that her Hello Kitty cake was roadkill.

"You're staying here, Aunt Rosemary?" Julia asked, trying to play on the old woman's aversion to change. "Do you really think you'll be comfortable?"

"I suppose I will be." She grunted, then added, "Though it is a dreadful house."

Cassie began to cry, but Madelyn swept her into her lap and shushed her, and a heavy silence filled the formal room. Julia didn't think it was possible for ten five-year-olds to be so silent at a birthday party, but it was happening. Everyone just stared at the cake that lay burning at Caroline's feet, a pile of chocolate and frosting on her pristine floor.

"Happy birthday to you," Lance began singing. Julia looked at him as if he was crazy, but he motioned for her to sing along. "Happy birthday to you!" they sang together. Soon, everyone but Caroline and Ro-Ro had joined in—Georgia B. providing the alto.

Later, when the crowd cleared and exhausted children were carried away in their parents' arms, Steve and Nina began disposing of the wrapping paper and ribbons. Madelyn went upstairs to put baby Nick down for a nap, and Caroline was on her knees, scrubbing away what was left of Hello Kitty.

Julia dropped beside her and whispered, "It's almost over."

Her sister's hands never stopped scrubbing as she said, "I can't *believe* my daughter had to blow out the floor."

"Caroline, I'm going to have to go home with Lance. . . . What am I going to do?"

"What are *you* going to do?" Caroline blew hair out of her face with a puff. "You have *got* to be kidding me. You have a kind and handsome houseguest. I"—Caroline paused for effect—"have Ro-Ro. Julia, you are on your own."

# Chapter Eleven

Julia imagined saying, "Sorry, you have to go to a hotel." But it was too late; Lance already had the bags out of the trunk and sitting on her front porch. He stood behind her, waiting for her to unlock the door.

Cool, damp air blew in from the creek, carrying the aroma of dogwoods in bloom, but the porch light didn't reach the creek bank, so the delicate white flowers stayed eclipsed by the night. She wished Lance could see the way the house settled in the low, rolling hills. Visitors always commented on the serenity of the land—the ultimate first impression.

Not this time.

"Love what you've done with the place," he said once they'd stepped inside.

*Sarcasm?* Julia wondered, looking around at the chipped paint and sagging floors of the foyer and the living room, studying Lance with fresh eyes. *I can respect sarcasm,* she decided.

The floors creaked as Lance and Julia walked through her home—her one romantic notion. Built by a district court judge in the days of Indian Territory, the white two-story house deserved better than rot and decay. She'd remodeled the kitchen and master bath in order to make the house livable. Those rooms alone had taken a full year of worrying over every pull, knob, and tile. Nina had quit the project, saying no self-respecting interior decorator would work with someone like Julia, best friend or not. In the back of her mind, Julia realized that Nina was right, and if she completed only one room every two years, she'd finish the house just in time for Cassie and Nick to inherit it from her. Still, she didn't have the fortitude to tackle any more, and she'd grown accustomed to the sparse surroundings.

Standing there with Lance Collins, however, made Julia regret not making more of an effort. As she looked at his nearly perfect face, she couldn't help but imagine that he lived in a nearly perfect home. She saw the layers of dust that hadn't bothered her before, and she wished she'd at least cleaned the floor before going on tour.

"I'm sorry it's not . . ." she began, but Lance held out a hand to stop her.

"It's fine. Really, it's got a lot of . . ."

"Charm?" she guessed.

"Potential."

"You may not be a bad actor after all," she answered his lie.

"That's what I keep trying to tell everyone!" he exclaimed, and Julia welcomed the moment of levity. "What's that beeping noise?" he asked, and Julia bolted to the kitchen where she punched a code into an alarm box on the wall by the back door. When she turned, she saw him leaning against the island.

"Do you really need that out here?" he asked.

Julia could see his point. Aside from the hum of the refrigerator, there wasn't a solitary sound. She remembered the honking and sirens that filled even the most peaceful New York night. Her old house must seem like the middle of nowhere to him, the kind of place where people were fighting to get out, not trying to break in. She shrugged and said, "Too much silence can be scarier than too much noise."

To her relief, he nodded and said, "Yeah, I know what you mean."

His quiet smile threw her suddenly off guard. She nervously threw open the refrigerator door. "Can I get you something to drink?" she asked, lapsing into hostess mode. "Maybe a pop, some cheese? I have some excellent cheese."

"No," he said quietly, stepping closer, forcing Julia toward the open refrigerator. The cold blasted her from behind. "Bed."

"Excuse me?"

"I think I need to go to bed. For tonight, Julia, I'm going to have to pass on the cheese."

♠

"So does he still respect you this morning?" Nina said instead of hello.

Julia hung up on her.

While waiting for Nina to call back, she realized she hadn't even seen Lance yet. She'd overslept . . . again. Cursing insomnia . . . again. By the time she'd undergone a little obligatory primping, it was after ten, and he was nowhere to be seen.

"Okay, okay. Point taken," Nina said as soon as Julia answered. "You're touchy. I can empathize. So, really, how's it going?"

"The truth is, I don't know. I haven't seen him." Then she saw the empty hook by the back door. "My keys are gone!" She jogged to the living room and looked out the window. "My car is gone!" she said, and began running through the house. "Where's my purse? Did he steal my purse?"

"Julia, calm down," Nina said through the phone. "Do you really think someone would fly halfway across the country to steal your purse? I have seen your purse, and frankly, you could use an upgrade."

"Nina," Julia started. Then, through the front windows, she saw her car crest the hill and proceed slowly down the long, winding driveway. She followed it, watching as it circled around to the back of the house and parked by the kitchen door. "I'm gonna have to call you back."

"Hey," Lance said a moment later when he walked through the back door carrying two brown paper bags. "Good morning. I borrowed your car. Hope you don't mind. You didn't have much in the fridge, and I wanted to . . ."

His voice trailed off as Julia's gaze went to the black tips of his fingers—newsprint. He took a slight step toward her and said, "How about breakfast? I got—"

She finished for him. "You got some newspapers."

He didn't reply.

"Show me," she said, holding out a hand.

He reached into one of the bags, but before handing anything over, he asked, "Do you want the good news or the bad news?"

"There's good news?" she asked, amazed.

He pulled out two tabloids and handed them to her. The headline on top read: WHERE ARE LANCE AND JULIA?

Lance pulled an apple from one of the bags, rubbed it on his sleeve, and took a bite. A small trickle of juice ran from the corner of his mouth as he spoke and gestured toward the paper with the forbidden fruit. "They don't have a clue where we are. Evidently, we've been spotted around the globe. That one says Barbados." A sly grin slid onto his lips as he licked juice from the corner of his mouth. "I think we've lost them."

The relief almost knocked Julia off her feet. A sudden whoosh of air swept into her lungs. *Freedom*, she wanted to sing as she ran barefoot through Easter lilies. She wanted to re-create entire numbers from *Grease*. She was an Old Navy commercial just looking for a place to happen.

As the apple core hit the bottom of the trash can, the *thunk* drew her out of her daydream. Lance's hand reached back into the bag, and Julia remembered that there was more to the story.

"The bad news is . . . well . . . we're still news."

# Chapter Twelve

It never ceased to amaze Julia what strangers will do in a woman's kitchen. During the remodel, Julia had complained that they were making the room too large. *I don't want to run a marathon every time I need something from the freezer,* she remembered saying. But Nina had cocked her head and said, "Kitchens are the new living rooms," and insisted on the additional space. Now, with Lance continually under foot, Julia was starting to believe Nina was a genius.

Watching him, she knew he probably wouldn't dare re-arrange her underwear drawer, but here he was, trying to

wedge a gallon of milk into the Diet Coke shelf of the refrigerator door.

"That doesn't go there," she said, trying to remember if
there had ever been an entire gallon of milk in her refrigerator.
She was pretty sure there hadn't. "That's going to go bad, you
know," she couldn't stop herself from saying. "I can't use a
whole gallon of milk before it goes bad."

"Maybe you can't," Lance said, "but we can."

The "we" hit her hard. She scanned the kitchen island
where he'd emptied the bags and saw white bread, guacamole,
and full-calorie pop—all three signs of the apocalypse. Then
came the straw that broke the camel's back: the plastic mon-
strosity in Lance's hands was whole milk.

"Whole milk!" Julia said, appalled. When Lance looked at
her, she threw her hands to Heaven and said, "Skim!" Then
she got out of the kitchen.

In the living room later in the day, things only got worse.

*One television set plus two virtual strangers must be a
recipe for disaster,* Julia thought, realizing she should probably
write down that pearl of wisdom—it would make a great chapter for a book someday. As Lance zoomed through seventy-five
channels at Olympic-record pace, she thought she could now
understand a little of what married women go through. His
underwear hadn't appeared on the bathroom floor yet, but one
could only assume it was just a matter of time.

*That's assuming he wears underwear,* her inner Nina
chimed, so Julia went outside to take a head-clearing walk.

When she came back, Lance had settled on a station. It was ESPN Classic. *Where is the suspense in watching something that happened twenty years ago?* When he said, "I remember this game!" it took every ounce of her restraint not to say, "Then why do you need to watch it again?"

Instead, Julia settled herself in the comfy chair and picked up a book. She consoled herself by realizing that at least when he was watching TV, he wasn't walking around on her creaky floorboards, making more noise than a marching band, disturbing the blessed stillness of her quiet house. Even on the couch, however, he still managed to shatter her peace with the perpetual shaking of ice cubes in his glass of Coke. *Full-calorie* Coke. Julia winced and Lance asked, "What's wrong?"

"Nothing. I'm just not used to other people's noise."

He looked at her as though she'd just told him she kept a UFO in the basement, then went right back to cheering for a team he already knew was going to lose.

She shivered and began to regret telling him where to find the thermostat. Sun streamed through the windows, and outside it had to be near eighty, yet the house was a brisk sixty-nine. She wanted her chenille afghan, but it was beneath his beefy leg.

"You've got to watch this shot," he said as he held the remote control like a magic wand that he could use to manipulate the players. "Wait, it's coming up," he said. "It's coming . . . it's . . ."

The doorbell rang, so Julia had to miss whatever play had

happened so many years before. She went to the door and looked through the peephole, thinking it would be Nina or Caroline.

"Yoo-hoo!"

Miss Georgia's drawl was like sugar dissolving in tea.

"Anybody home?"

With one eye glued to the peephole, the surrealness of her life was starting to seep in. There was a man spread across the couch behind her and a porch full of Georgias in front of her. Julia had never felt so trapped. The doorbell rang again and she felt Lance come to stand behind her. "Press?" he asked.

She shook her head, turned the dead bolt, and opened the door.

Pink must have been the color of the day because the Georgias were all decked out in different derivations of the shade: Miss Georgia in fuchsia, Georgia A. in baby-girl, and Georgia B. in magenta. Standing together and leaning forward with grins on their faces, grasping their coordinating handbags, they looked like a float in the Rose Parade, something titled "Tickled Pink."

"Don't you all look nice!" Julia said, remembering her upbringing.

Georgia A. was all smiles as she said, "We tried calling, but your phone must be off the hook."

"I was afraid we might get some unsettling calls," Julia admitted, a little guilty about that decision.

"Oh, darling," Miss Georgia jumped in. "You don't owe us any explanation. When I was in the Miss America pageant, I had my line disengaged for three weeks. I know *exactly* what you're saying."

"Thank you," Julia said. Noticing the way the three pink flowers seemed to be wilting in the sun, she felt compelled to add, "Won't you come in?" They didn't waste one second before plowing past her toward Lance, who was standing between the door and the stairs.

Georgia B. looked him up and down, then said to Miss Georgia, "I think it's going to fit. Don't you, Evelyn?" Only then did Julia notice the garment bag that Miss Georgia had draped over one of her impossibly well-toned arms. Miss Georgia answered, "I think it might."

Georgia A. turned to Julia and explained: "When we got home yesterday evening, we remembered that Lance wouldn't have known to pack his tuxedo," she said in a "we're so silly" tone of voice, and Julia remembered that the Georgias are not regular people.

Georgia A. continued, saying, "Of course, when I was your age, a man never traveled without at least one formal suit, but I know that times have changed."

*Oh, Georgia,* Julia thought, *you have no idea.*

Miss Georgia had taken a tux jacket out of the garment bag and was helping Lance slip it on. The Georgias stood back and admired him as Lance worked his arms back and forth, trying out the fit.

"How does that feel?" Georgia B. asked. "Not too snug, I hope?"

"No," Lance said and grinned at her. "It's perfect."

There were congratulations all around as the Georgias stood in Julia's living room, looking excessively proud of themselves. Julia was taken aback when she saw tears swelling in Georgia B.'s eyes. "Georgia," she said, "what's wrong?"

"Oh, nothing, dear," she said while dabbing at her eyes with a pink handkerchief. "It's just that Rosemary would be so proud to see this."

Julia couldn't believe her ears. *Aunt Rosemary thought of this?* She couldn't think of a single time in history when Ro-Ro had done anything for anyone. She certainly couldn't remember Ro-Ro shelling out to buy something that must have cost as much as that tuxedo. "*Rosemary* bought Lance a tuxedo?" Julia asked, disbelieving.

"No, dear," Georgia B. said, still dabbing at her eyes. "This was Wally's old tux—the one he wore to their wedding. Yesterday, when she realized how similar he and Lance were, she decided that someone should be getting some good out of it."

So, okay, Ro-Ro had given Lance a sixty-year-old tuxedo—that was more like it. But it was still the favorite tux of her favorite husband, and that fact struck Julia to the bone.

"A cut like that never goes out of style," Georgia A. said, admiring the jacket. "My William had at least twenty tuxedos in his life, and the first one he owned was more in style when he died than the last one he bought. Wally was the same way. Men like that are timeless."

Julia had to admit, Georgia A. had a point.

Like a magnet, her hand was drawn to a piece of nonexistent lint on Lance's shoulder. Her fingers lingered a little longer than she had intended, and Lance suddenly grabbed her wrist. He put his other arm around her waist and pulled her tightly to him. Electric sparks sizzled up and down her spine. *It's the rug,* Julia told herself, *definitely static charge*. Then, with one fluid, effortless motion, he dipped her low, and her whole world turned upside down. He moved closer and closer, until his face was only inches away. His lips parted as he said, "Wanna go to a party?"

"Yes!" a chorus of high voices cried out.

Julia turned her head to see three pink figures looming overhead, smiling.

# Chapter Thirteen

"Sycamore Hills," Lance said, pondering it. "Where have I heard that before?"

"Golf," Julia answered as she steered onto a cobblestone lane, past a guardhouse, and between the eighth and seventeenth fairways. She heard her inner golf announcer whisper, *They're passing through the magnolia groves now, Bob, a dogleg to the right. No wind to speak of. Two hundred yards to the clubhouse and . . . oh, yes, she's doing it in second gear.*

Lance asked, "Was the PGA tour here in 2000 or 2001?"

"I really don't know," Julia answered. *And don't care,*

she thought. But no matter how much the game bored her, she couldn't deny the beauty of its stage. Sunlight glistened off ponds as daylight fought for its hold on the horizon. The plantation-style clubhouse looked like Tara itself, surrounded by manicured lawns. The whole world seemed Technicolor gorgeous as the valet held Julia's door and Lance came to stand beside her. She stopped for a moment, looking up at the wide portico stairs that, like Jack's beanstalk, led to another world—one designed for giants of industry, lazy trust-fund brats, and Georgias. A world where no matter how many best-sellers she wrote, Julia had never belonged.

That is, until she walked in on the arm of Lance Collins.

Climbing the stairs on the arm of a handsome man in a vintage tuxedo, Julia saw Sycamore Hills in an entirely different light. She felt the eyes of strangers on her, a feeling she knew, but the gazes somehow seemed different. These weren't the *Don't I know her?* or *Isn't she famous?* looks she'd been getting since *Table for One* debuted. They certainly weren't the *What's wrong with her?* looks she'd been getting for far longer. These were *Oh, what a lovely couple* looks, Julia was sure. She jerked her head, trying to see behind her, wondering if she was only standing in between those complimentary glances and the woman they were really for. But no, the only person back there was Archie Givens, a man whose children had once hired an attorney to keep him away from Ro-Ro.

*We're the best-looking people in here,* Julia thought,

bolstered by the revelation. *Of course, we're also forty years younger. . . .* But she still couldn't help feeling like a Bond girl.

When she saw her least-favorite employee rushing toward them, Julia readied herself for the evening's ultimate test: This was a man who could make supermodels feel fat, and heads of state inferior. He screeched to a halt in front of them and, to Julia's amazement, smiled.

"Good evening, ma'am," he said to Julia. "Sir," he addressed Lance. "Welcome to Sycamore Hills. And whom will you be meeting this evening?" he asked, even though Julia knew he was well aware of who she was. Still, he held tight to his podium and his questions, refusing to let anyone or anything rip that power from his bony hands.

"We're the guests of Rosemary Willis," Julia told him, mustering a smile.

"Excellent," he said, his eyes scanning a list. "Table twenty-seven. Ma'am," he asked, "may I check your wrap?"

Julia looked at her emerald-green shoulder wrap. History told her never to surrender layers when entering the Sycamore Hills ballroom, because while Ro-Ro's crowd didn't believe in skimping on the curtains, they weren't about to turn up the heat. "No, thank you."

"Very well. Enjoy your evening." He ended the statement with a smile, not his usual look of scorn for Julia the dateless leper. Julia felt herself nearly floating toward the ballroom at the rear of the building through a corridor of twenty-foot ceilings and more crown molding than a palace, and she couldn't resist stealing a glance at Lance.

"So, what do you think?"

He let out a low whistle in response.

Since meeting Lance, Julia had covered the full range of emotions, from calm serenity to blinding panic, and now she felt herself looping around to giddy. A sudden burst of laughter shot out of her so fast that she threw her hand to her lips as if to catch the laugh and cram it back down her throat.

"What?" he said. "What is it?" He pulled his hands to his face and started wiping away nonexistent crumbs.

Another giggle from Julia.

"Stop laughing," he said.

But it was out of her control. "Look at us," she said between fits, as regally dressed older couples inched past them, pushing walkers and dragging oxygen tanks. "Would you *look* at us?" She held her hands away from her body so he could get the full effect. Then she leaned closer and said, "We're on the *lam—in formal wear*. I thought this kind of thing only happened on *Days of Our Lives*."

"Sweetheart, don't take this the wrong way," he said, a grin on his lips as he placed her hand through his arm and began steering her toward the ballroom, "but you're a little loopy."

"Maybe so," she said, "but at least I'm not wearing a dead man's tuxedo."

Actually, she was wearing an old bridesmaid dress, but the less Lance knew about that, the better.

The hallway widened as they reached four sets of double doors leading into the ballroom. A portrait hung on the wall of the circular room. Lance looked at the painting and then read from the placard beneath it: WALLIFORD "WALLY" WILLIS. SYCAMORE HILLS PRESIDENT, 1939–1942.

"So that's the famous Wally," he said, as if meeting a long-lost friend.

"Don't worry." She brushed the lapel of his jacket. "You look better in the tux."

Lance leaned forward and studied the painting of the great-uncle Julia never knew. She and Caroline had frequently wondered what Ro-Ro's favorite husband must have been like. Was he strong enough to stand up to her, or weak enough to let her win every fight? Looking at the painting, Julia realized she'd known the answer all along. Wally must have been strong—very strong. There were plenty of people who were willing to cave in to Ro-Ro, but few who were worthy opponents. Julia studied the sharp, lean man in the picture, and she realized he hadn't just been her great love, he'd been her great challenge and, for Ro-Ro, the two were cosmically linked.

"He died young," Lance said, gesturing to the bio that hung beside the frame.

Julia nodded. "They weren't married for very long, and they lived abroad most of that time. When they moved home, he spent most of his days here." She gestured at their opulent surroundings. "And then he suddenly died. I think she hates this place because of it."

Lance nodded. "My dad spent all his time away, too. My mom hated him for it."

"Oh," Julia said. "I'm sorry. I didn't realize your father had passed away."

"He's hasn't," Lance told her. "But my parents divorced, and he dropped off the face of the earth. The man's still living. But the father's dead."

And then something dawned on Julia. "I really don't know anything about you," she said. "What's your mother's name?"

"Donna."

"What does she do for a living?"

"She manages theater companies, anywhere and everywhere that will have her. She's great at it."

"Do you have any brothers or sisters?"

"It was just me and my mom."

"Let's see," Julia said, struggling to think of more questions. "I already know you like whole milk and full-calorie pop—does everyone in your family have good metabolisms?"

A wide smile spread across Lance's face. "Yes."

"Too bad. I was just starting to like you."

♣

"Jules, you look magnificent!" Caroline cried when they neared Ro-Ro's table. Even Steve seemed to take notice as he stood to kiss her cheek and shake Lance's hand.

"Turn around," Caroline said. "Let me look at your dress."

"Caroline, *you* picked it out."

"I know, but I don't remember it being this stunning on you."

The black gown was floor-length with an empire waist, a simple scoop-neck collar, and an emerald-green wrap. Seven years and eight pounds ago, the dress had been Julia's idea of perfection. As she eased into a chair between Lance and Caroline, she wondered if it might still have the golden touch.

Right up until the point when Nina showed up wearing it.

Halfway through the silent auction, Julia looked up from the table to see her best friend floating through the geriatric ocean like a feather on the tide—a feather wrapped in emerald green. Julia's mouth gaped. Instinctively, she looked around the table, wondering if Lance or any of the others had seen. She said a silent prayer of thanks that they were all listening to Steve talk about tax-sheltered annuity limits, and no one had noticed Nina, who stood frozen on the dance floor, obviously unsure what to do.

"Excuse me," Julia said. "I'm going to run to the ladies' room."

She gave Nina a look, pointed to the powder room, and sprinted there herself. As soon as she'd checked for feet beneath the stall doors, Julia hissed, "What are you wearing?"

"My bridesmaid dress from Caroline's wedding?" Nina asked, as if it might be a trick question.

Julia smacked her on the shoulder. "You've got to go home and change!"

"Me? Why do *I* have to go home?"

"Because you live five minutes from here. I live sixty miles away!" Julia scolded.

"I can't," Nina admitted. "I don't have anything else to wear."

"Neither do I," Julia shot back.

"Well, I can't leave!" Nina said, anticipating what Julia was going to say next. "There's too much potential business in that room. Plus, I can't tell Jason he rented a tux for nothing."

Julia froze, dumbfounded. Could she have heard that correctly? "You're here with *Jason*?"

"Well, I couldn't come by *myself*. And he called last night—"

"Nina, I cannot believe you're here with him."

"Jules, it's okay. We're here as friends."

"Like you went on vacation to Vegas together as friends?" Julia mocked. "I seem to remember you coming home from that one *remarried*."

"So what about us wearing the same dress, huh? This is pretty embarrassing."

"Nina, don't change the subject!" Julia snapped.

The door opened and Julia heard Caroline say, "I thought I'd see what was taking you—oh my gosh!" She gasped as she turned the corner. "Oh my gosh. Oh my gosh." Caroline was rocking back and forth in a manner that suggested that as the bride, she should have seen this coming. "When I said you could wear the dresses again," she exclaimed, "I didn't mean at the same time!"

"Caroline," Julia said, "we have bigger problems. Jason is—"

"Yoo-hoo!"

Georgia A. led the gang around the corner, then stopped, clasped her hands together in front of her elegantly age-appropriate gown, and said, "The gentlemen said that you ladies had locked yourselves up in here. I think we've figured out *why*."

Julia took one look at Miss Georgia in a royal-blue ribbon of a dress with a slit down the side revealing one stunning leg and she went to stand by Georgia B., who looked like she'd bought her dress from army surplus. Georgia B. put her arms around Julia and said, "Don't worry, sweetheart, we're going to work something out."

"I think I'll just go home," Julia found herself saying. "I should have just stayed home. I should have . . ." Julia couldn't believe it; she was honestly starting to cry. Standing in the bathroom of Sycamore Hills, wearing a bridesmaid dress, surrounded by Georgias, she was crying. *Julia James doesn't cry,* she thought. *Julia James is a bestselling author, one of the most bankable names in books! Julia's fans know her as someone who is calm and confident, ready for whatever curves life throws her!*

She cursed Ro-Ro for making her come. She cursed Lance for making it so wonderful for a few minutes. She cursed the fact that once you get used to floating into rooms, it hurts a lot more to crawl out.

"Oh, honey," Miss Georgia was saying. "This simply will not do."

"I know that, Evelyn," Julia stammered. "That's why I'm crying."

Caroline massaged her sister's shoulders. "It's okay, honey. Shhhh." Then Caroline turned to the Georgias. "She's been under so much pressure lately, with the reporters and all the rumors. I'm surprised she's held up as well as she has."

"Honey." Julia heard Miss Georgia's sweet drawl. "You're doing terrible things to your makeup. There's no use making us fix what wasn't broken to begin with."

"Fix?" Julia brushed her hair out of her eyes.

"*Of course,*" the Georgias sang in unison.

"Now, let's look at both of you," Georgia A. said, pushing Nina closer to Julia. "Ladies, what do you think?"

Miss Georgia planted her hands on her nearly nonexistent hips and said, "Julia has been here longer, so more people have seen her. She will be harder to change."

"But little Nina is so perfect in that gown. Oh, it would be a pity to touch it," Georgia B. said, and Julia no longer thought she was the nice one. But then Georgia B. redeemed herself by saying, "Plus, I don't think that neckline does Julia justice. It should accentuate her stately shoulders and show her wonderful skin."

"Agreed," Miss Georgia said.

"Wait!" Julia held out a hand. "Caroline, did you know Nina is here with Jason?"

"Yes. He's already at the table. You should have seen the tension between him and Lance when I left—very *National Geographic.*"

*Now this I've got to see,* Julia thought, but then she caught a glimpse of herself in the mirror and immediately the dread came rushing back. "I can't walk out there in a different dress. That's going to be too weird."

"Has anyone seen you without the wrap, dear?" Georgia A. asked.

"Well, no," Julia had to concede.

The Georgias all seemed to exhale, and Miss Georgia started toward her. "It's settled then. A lot of women are wearing black dresses, darling. We'll simply reverse Nina's wrap and change your neckline," Miss Georgia said. Then she dumped her small bag onto the makeup vanity, and a whole beauty arsenal fell out.

Twenty minutes later, Julia emerged from the bathroom with a different neckline and an entirely new appreciation for what a former Miss Georgia could do with cuticle scissors and double-sided tape.

Lance watched the way the waiter cleared from the right and served from the left, the way he moved noiselessly, effortlessly between the seated couples, and he realized that this man was no actor-in-waiting; this man was a pro. Only decades of experience within the Sycamore Hills ballroom could give a man the fortitude he would need to keep an even expression on his face as Jason ordered.

"Bring me the pork with the steamed rice instead of the

potatoes, and the vegetable medley instead of the salad, and coffee with skim milk, not cream. You getting this down?" Jason asked the man, who looked old enough to have been hired by Wally Willis himself.

Maybe it was Lance's imagination, but as the waiter turned, he thought the man might have given him a wink. Lance smiled, relieved to be among peers, glad for the chance to see things from that side of the table for a change, even if it did mean sitting across from Jason. At least he got to share the table with Julia.

One June, while working the wedding-reception circuit, Lance had developed a theory that there are two kinds of people in the world—the kind who say thank you when you refill their glass, and the kind who act as if the water has miraculously reappeared. Julia, Lance decided halfway through the meal, was a thanker. Each and every time someone refilled a glass or removed or placed a plate, Julia said "thank you" in the perfect volume, the perfect tone. He'd served a lot of people, but he'd never seen anyone hit a hundred percent—until Julia. When Julia said thank you for her salmon and Jason decided that his pork needed to go back to the kitchen, Lance realized that Julia James was his kind of woman.

"So, you're an actor, Lance," Jason said. "That's pretty unstable work."

Lance nodded and said, "It can be."

"I'm in sales. Top in my district, three years running."

*So this is our game,* Lance thought, deciding it was as good as any. After all, Lance couldn't see a basketball hoop any-where, and the Sycamore Hills people probably wouldn't appreciate them arm wrestling near the good crystal. "Very impressive," Lance said, sliding his sarcasm directly under Jason's nose.

Jason gave an "aw, shucks" shrug of his shoulders. "Clos-ing deals comes easier for me than most people. I visualize scoring—like in football. You play any ball, Lance?"

"No," Lance said, adjusting the napkin on his lap. "Not competitively."

"Oh, well, nothing to be ashamed of, buddy. Someone's got to sit in the stands and cheer." Jason smiled. "Isn't that right, Tiny?" he asked, turning to Nina, who wore the grin of a game-show contestant who couldn't believe the parting gift was such a prize.

*Is this the same woman who drove her VW on the shoulder of the road and passed a semi doing ninety?* Lance wanted to ask. The look on Nina's face made him feel sick. The sight must have bothered Julia, too, because Lance felt her tense and ask, "So, Jason, how's the house hunting going?"

"Renting works fine for me," Jason said before taking a bite of the pork he'd finally accepted. "I'm keeping my options open."

"Yeah," Julia said. "I know how much you like your *options*."

Lance thought he could almost hear Julia thinking, *But Nina is not for rent.*

Next to Julia, Caroline put her fork down with a clank. "Have I told you about my new Swiffer? It's just amaz—"

"I'm not sure I really need to buy a place." Jason sliced through Caroline's words as if she didn't exist. He was holding Nina's hand, looking deeply into her eyes.

"Jason, it's a *great* time to buy," Julia exclaimed. "I hear Owasso is nice. Why don't you move to Owasso?"

"Has anybody seen the new Remington exhibit?" Caroline blurted. "I hear it's—"

"Owasso is completely on the other side of town!" Nina jumped in.

Caroline picked up the basket on the table and said, "Who wants bread?"

"I realize that," Julia said, glaring at her best friend. "The *distance* might be good. It might make it easier to *move on*," she finished, brandishing her fork until Lance covered her hand with his, hoping to stop her from leaning across the table and taking out one of Jason's eyes.

"Sunken treasure!" Caroline yelled, and everyone at three tables turned to her. "I saw the most interesting documentary about sunken treasure," she said, and spent the rest of the main course retelling it in detail without even pausing for breath until their plates were cleared and the emcee announced that people had just five minutes until the silent auction closed.

The crowd began to stir while dessert was being served, and Lance noticed the noise level in the room creep a little higher as the free booze started to mix with the heart medication that was, no doubt, filling two-thirds of the tuxedo pockets in the room. Nina and Caroline slipped off to feel the drapes. Jason excused himself to go call a customer. Steve was at another table, consoling a client about some loophole that Congress had just closed, leaving Lance and Julia at the table alone when the band eased seamlessly into more danceable music.

Lance looked at Julia, the gorgeous curve of her neck, the look of concern she wore for everyone she loved. He realized he had been acting for most of his adult life, but he didn't know who to be right then. Maybe it was Wally's old tuxedo, or the grandeur of Sycamore Hills, but he was having a very hard time acting like himself. He started to ask her to dance, but then drew back, suddenly unsure of his line.

From the corner of his eye, he saw a royal-blue vision floating toward their table.

"Julia, darling," Miss Georgia said, distressed. "No one's dancing. These events are marked as complete and utter failures if no one dances. Come," she said, taking Julia's arm. "You and Lance have to dance. When people see you, they'll join in."

"Oh, Evelyn, I don't really think—"

"Julia, *please*," Miss Georgia pleaded. "Please, do this for me."

Julia looked at Lance. "Do you want to dance?"

He rose and said, "I thought you'd never ask."

Before she could recant, he led her onto the dance floor and pulled her into his arms. *Oh, man,* he thought, *she smells good.* When he felt the soft skin on her back, he thought, *She feels good, too.* Then he stepped on her toe.

"Sorry," he muttered, but Julia just smiled.

When the band changed tempo, they found their rhythm. Lance breathed her in, stealing little glances as Julia looked into the crowd. "Julia," he whispered. He felt himself get tongue-tied. "I liked the pork."

She raised her eyebrows and said, "Good. They have great chefs here."

*I liked the pork?* Lance berated himself as they fell into awkward silence. "I hate Jason," he said, grasping for common ground.

At this, Julia exhaled and momentarily dropped her cheek onto his shoulder. "Promise you won't let me kill him. Just promise me I won't end up in jail twice in one week."

Lance laughed, and with his old smile, his old confidence returned. Their steps became more fluid, and soon they were floating across the floor. When he spun her out and smoothly back into his arms, he told her, "I'm an old-fashioned guy, Julia. I'd be more than happy to do the killing for you."

"You're not just saying that to get on my good side?"

"No, I hate him."

Julia smiled, and she looked like he hadn't seen her look since that first day in the cab, as if she was comfortable in her own skin, certain of where she was going. For the first time since they'd arrived in Oklahoma, Julia looked at home.

◆

On the ride back to her place, Julia let Lance drive. He had taken off the tuxedo jacket and loosened his tie, and as they drove down the gravel road, she studied him in the glow of the dashboard lights. He looked like he belonged on a billboard in Times Square, or in a cologne commercial. He seemed too perfect to be real. So when they reached the house, Julia hurried inside, anxious to be tucked safely in bed before the clock struck twelve and she turned back into a pumpkin.

"I'm going to bed," she said.

"You are? It's not even that late," he protested, and she knew he was right. Ro-Ro's events were always of the early-bird variety; it was still before eleven.

"I'm exhausted, really. Just make yourself at home and . . ."

The phone rang. Julia, too exhausted to think clearly, answered it. "Hello?"

"Julia, honey, Richard Stone here. How's our boy?"

Julia froze; the night came to a grinding halt. Lance read her gaze as she stared at the receiver. He took the phone from her hand and killed the line.

"It was Richard Stone," she said numbly. "He wanted you."

"You didn't tell him I was here, Julia," he said.

"But you *are* here. You're in my house. It's going to look like—"

"Julia." He spun her to face him. "Things are okay. Okay? Look at me. How much property do you have here?"

"Almost five hundred acres. I rent it. I mean, I let my dad run cows on it."

"How many roads are there to the house?"

"Just the one, the main one. There's a county road on one side, but other than that, we're landlocked."

"Okay, good. We're on private property as long as we're here. The press can't come near us. We can call the sheriff if we have to, but they can't set foot on your property."

His arms were on her shoulders. His voice was soft but strong when he said, "No one has proof we're together, but they're probably coming to get some."

"Yes."

"This changes things," he said.

"I know."

# Chapter Fourteen

> **WAY #15: Don't let little things get you down.**
> It's important to keep life in perspective. Comments from people who don't know or understand you should never make you question your own worth. After all, you are the world's greatest expert on yourself.
>
> —from *101 Ways to Cheat at Solitaire*

The clock on the bedside table kept ticking—not an unfamiliar sound. But that night, the cards didn't seem to soothe Julia's mind. She wrapped her arms around her knees and tried not to think about the man in the bedroom down the hall. She tried not to imagine the headlines that would swell as soon as the tabloids learned that he was in her house, sleeping under her roof. Reporters and photographers were certainly on their way, so Julia pulled the cards back together and slipped them into their cardboard box, knowing the situation wouldn't change, no matter how thoroughly she shuffled.

She pulled on a robe and slippers and moved quietly into the hallway, past the closed door of Lance's room. The shades on the window in the upstairs landing were drawn so tightly that not even the moon crept into the dark house, yet she feared turning on a light, as if, right then, men with telescopic lenses were perched in the limbs of sycamore trees, trying to invade her home. She trusted the smooth surface of the mahogany banister to guide her down the stairs. When she reached the foyer, she turned into a small room, slid the big double doors as far as they would go, and sealed herself away from everything beyond the four walls of her home office. She went to the desk where her computer waited, pushed the button, and heard the machine chime to life.

Her house might be four miles from the nearest neighbor, its walls might be thick, the woods might be dense, but Julia knew chaos could intrude on these comfortable borders. She had returned home to block herself off from the outside world, but her career was still going on without her—*out there*. The sales figures Candon had given her that day at the Ritz were *astronomical*. He'd known how those sales would translate into income. As the Windows icon flashed on the screen, Julia looked around her study with its broken shelves and cracking walls and asked the room itself, "Does it *look* like I'm in it for the money?"

*Surely the momentum is bound to swing*, she told herself as she typed in the URL for Amazon.com and wondered if she was the only writer in history to hope that her sales ranking had plummeted.

It hadn't.

Next, Julia directed the browser to an Internet search engine. She held her breath as she typed "Julia James" and "Lance Collins" into the query field, and clicked *Go*. Soon she found herself looking at results one through twenty of 250,000. To make matters worse, the banner at the top of the screen said that she was the most searched-for item of the week. *It's official*, Julia thought. *I am utterly and completely Googled*.

She clicked on the first link and read until the words were burned into her mind.

WHAT WILL WOMEN DO NOW? THE NEW STATE OF SINGLE by a columnist at a national daily that had weather predictions, box scores, and a place on the lobby counter at every hotel in America.

With bestselling author Julia James off the market, single women, psychologists, and cultural analysts are all asking the same question: Will single ever be the same?

From the time *Table for One* debuted five years ago, Julia James has been the face of the single woman. But since she and boyfriend Lance Collins were photographed on a New York street in the shot heard around the world, fans and critics alike are calling her career into question.

"She's a fraud," says Maria Snider, who once chaired the Albany, New York, chapter of the Julia James Appreciation Society. "I paid my twenty-five bucks," she says, holding up a copy of the runaway bestseller *101 Ways to Cheat at Solitaire*. "I bought it looking for a role model, but what I got was a phony. I want my money back."

But few share Snider's point of view. In the Albany chapter of the JJAS alone, splinter groups have formed. Some, like Snider, long for the Julia of old. But most see this new chapter of their heroine's life as a testament to the power of true love.

Competing picket lines formed outside a bookstore in Chicago today, the "pro-relationship" faction brandishing signs and GIVE LANCE A CHANCE T-shirts. Others, like Snider, rallied behind cries of: "Table for one, not table for two. Lance, we have no use for you."

Controversy or not, sales for *101 Ways to Cheat at Solitaire* have been described by one industry insider as "mind-blowing."

"These are the same arguments about women's role in society we have seen since the end of the Second World War," said Peter Frisco, professor of Women's Studies at Columbia University. "Rosie the Riveter started it. Julia James is simply bringing it into the next century."

But the debate rages on. Has James abandoned her feminist credo, or has she simply followed her heart to another lifestyle choice? If this is the end of Julia James, this man wants to know what women will do without her on bookstands or in magazines telling them how to live. Without Julia, women may have to trust some other lifestyle guru—or, Heaven forbid, their hearts—to guide them.

"Thanks for coming," Lance said as he opened the door to Nina and Caroline. "I didn't know who else to call."

"What happened?" Caroline said. "You sounded upset on the phone."

"She's still up in her room," he said. "She won't come down. I didn't want to go in there, but . . ." He whispered, "I think she's crying."

Caroline and Nina took in quick, sharp gasps.

"I shouldn't have gone in, should I?" he asked, feeling utterly out of his league.

"Oh, good night, no!" Nina exclaimed. "*I* don't even want to go in." She gave Caroline a shove toward the stairs. "You go, C. You're her sister. She won't hurt someone who's lactating."

Caroline batted Nina's hands away and turned to Lance. "What happened?"

Lance moved to the club chair, and Nina and Caroline took seats on the couch. He ran his hands through his hair and said, "I'm really not sure. My agent called and asked for me. She hung up on him, didn't tell him a thing, but he pretty much knew I was here."

"So that sent her over to the dark side?" Nina asked.

"No, that's the thing. She was fine when she went to bed. Well, not fine really, but okay. When I came downstairs this morning, those doors were open." He pointed toward the study. "And I haven't seen her yet today."

Nina got up and went into the study, and Lance and Caroline followed through piles of books and past broken-down shelves. The windows had the aged look of old glass, a prism distorting the occupant's view of the world. The walls were covered with peeling paint and layers of old wallpaper that rippled from years of heat and humidity. The ceiling bore the stains of a room that has lived too long beneath a leaky roof. Everything smelled of neglect.

Caroline wrinkled her nose, "I don't know how she lives like this."

"Don't look at me," Nina said, throwing up her hands. "I stayed with her through nine months of decorating hell. I have more than paid my dues."

Lance guessed that Julia did all her writing in this room, and suddenly he felt wrong for being there. He realized that for Julia, the study must be as sacred and private as the master suite. "I don't think we should be in here," he said.

Nina waved him off. "If she wants to come downstairs and throw us out, that would suit me fine." She poked through papers on the desk: memos and letters, fan mail.

"The computer isn't on, is it?" Caroline asked.

"No," Lance said, "but the printer is."

♠

"Julia," Caroline said, knocking on her bedroom door. "Nina and I are here. Lance called us."

*Oh, no.* "Go away," Julia cried, trying to disguise her breaking throat. "Nothing's wrong. I just didn't sleep very well last night."

The door creaked open, and Caroline peered around the doorjamb. "Are you decent?" she asked softly, but Nina pushed past her.

"If not, you better get that way, because we're coming in." Nina plodded through the piles of dirty clothes that were scattered on the floor, overflowing out of open suitcases. She hopped onto the bed, flattening the duvet she'd given Julia for her thirtieth birthday, and asked, "What's your deal?" in a tone that suggested she wasn't going to let Julia mope the day away in any bed, no matter how beautiful its linens.

"I'm tired," Julia said, hoping that would end it.

But Caroline came in and, like Nina, crawled onto the queen-sized bed, and Julia heard the rustling of papers. Before she could stop her, Caroline reached into the pile of blankets and pulled the pages out. Caroline's eyes scanned the first sheet, and when she finished, she handed it to Nina and began reading the second.

"Wow," Caroline eventually said.

"Julia!" Nina exclaimed. "You're a T-shirt!"

*I've been on the* New York Times *bestseller list for five years, and this is what impresses Nina,* Julia thought and tumbled over onto the pillows. She felt Caroline stroke her hair, half expecting her to hold a tissue to her nose and say "blow" and then "good girl."

"When did I become the anti-relationship person?" Julia asked. "Caroline, did I try to talk you out of marriage? Nina . . ." She turned to the woman who had married Jason

twice, then rethought her question. "Well, you don't count."
Julia sat upright. "All I ever wanted was to help people make
the most out of the cards they've been dealt! Those were my
exact words!" she exclaimed, pointing a finger at no one in
particular. "Jeez! You tell Katie Couric something, and you
kind of expect the word to get around!"

"Julia," Caroline was saying, "this is something that happens. You read what that professor said. You didn't do this. It's
just a part of life." Tension was building in her voice. "Like
when the baby has colic and Cassie finger paints on the marble
in the guest bath. Stuff just happens!"

Julia took the article from Caroline, needing to feel it in
her hands to be sure she wasn't having a nightmare. "Half
my fans hate me! For no reason—I haven't abandoned them! I
haven't lied! I believe in what I wrote. Lance, whether he's
my *boyfriend*"—she choked out the word—"or not, doesn't
change that."

"But half your fans *love* you," Nina said.

Julia tossed off the covers. "No. Half of *her* fans love *her*!"
She pointed to the picture that had been taken that day outside
FAO Schwarz and included in every online news story about her
phenomenal success of the past week. "But she doesn't exist!"

"Well, for a ghost, she takes an excellent picture," Nina
chided.

"All I ever said was that marriage doesn't have to be everyone's cup of tea. Maybe tea's not available in your area.
Maybe you haven't found a flavor you like. Some people like

coffee. Some like pop. Some"—Julia felt her voice beginning to crack—"just try to avoid caffeine."

"So, you want us to leave," Nina said, rising to her knees on the bed. "You want us to leave so you can have a pity party—because some people you don't even know think you've got a *boyfriend*?" Nina got off the bed. "Jules, Caroline had a miscarriage last year. I've been divorced—twice—from the same guy. Ro-Ro, all joking aside, has buried four husbands. Forgive me, but the fact that you sold *a million* books in a week doesn't seem so very tragic."

With that, Nina whirled and walked to the door as quickly as her five-foot frame would allow. Minutes after she left, Caroline and Julia were both still sitting quietly on the bed, trying to adjust to Nina, the enforcer.

Julia hugged a pillow to her chest. "I don't know where I went so wrong," she said as she began to cry the big, fat tears that come only when the shutoff valve for emotion is broken. "It's so embarrassing. I'm just too embarrassed to be seen." She ran her pajama sleeve across her wet face.

Caroline shifted on the bed and turned to study her. "What do you mean?" she asked. "Why should you be embarrassed?"

"The snotty guy at Sycamore Hills was nice to me," Julia mumbled. "Miss Georgia fixed my dress. Ro-Ro made me go to that benefit, and you know she *never* would have done that if Lance hadn't been here to go with me." Tears were pouring out. "And now I see this!" She clenched the pages into her tight fists. "My sales have doubled. Why? *Because of him!*"

"Honey," Caroline said, "that's not true!"

"I'm just so ashamed," Julia said, wilting into soundless sobs.

Caroline let her get it all cried out before she asked, "Why, Julia? Why would you ever say such a thing?"

"I feel like people are looking at me now and saying, 'Oh, we're so *glad* there isn't something *wrong* with you.' That's what it feels like. Like people have thought there was something wrong with me for *years* but they're just admitting it *now*."

"Julia, you are reading way too much into this! All these people, your old fans and your new fans, they want to *be* you. They see this picture of you, smiling and laughing with a great-looking guy, so they go out to buy your books because they *want* that. You've proven it's possible. They've always wanted to be you, then and now. Everyone wants to be happy."

Julia looked at Caroline then, and something passed between them in the unspoken language of sisters. "Have you read the new book, Caroline?"

Her sister was quiet for a long time, then she said, "Don't lock yourself in your room, Julia. No one thought there was something wrong with you before, especially no one who knows you—not Ro-Ro, not the Georgias, not us."

"You're saying that if my friends and family hated me, they'd tell me to my face?"

Caroline pulled her sister's head onto her shoulder and smoothed her tangled hair. "Of course we would, sweetheart. Your friends are awful people."

# Chapter Fifteen

> **WAY #61: Don't be afraid to rearrange your life.**
> One of the marks of truly successful people is that they know
> how to change with the times, keep things fresh. If you feel
> yourself falling into a minor rut, make a minor change. If the
> feeling persists, it might be time to consider giving your life a
> fresh, new look.
>
> —from *101 Ways to Cheat at Solitaire*

"What if we move the bed over there?" Caroline pointed toward the wall that adjoined the master suite.

"No, trust me," Nina cut in. "You want to respect the symmetry of the room. We can't ignore the windows."

Julia stood on the upstairs landing and looked into the small room at the top of the stairs where her sister and best friend stood, hands on hips, like Lewis and Clark, mapping a way through the West.

"Well, whatever the case, we're getting new bedding," Caroline stated.

"Absolutely!" Nina jumped to agree.

Julia cleared her throat and watched Nina and Caroline turn to glare at her, as if they'd just found a secret stash of frozen cheesecakes that she'd been bringing to family re-unions, passing off as homemade. She stepped inside the small bedroom where Lance was leaning against the windowsill, an "I tried to stop them" expression on his face.

"Julia James!" Caroline snapped. "This is where you have this poor man sleeping? Have you even seen this room? How can you stand yourself?"

Julia hadn't given much thought to where Lance was stay-ing, but it was true that of all the rooms in the house, this one was in the worst shape. It was where she piled boxes of office supplies, out-of-style clothes, and things affectionately labeled "miscellaneous junk." The mess had never bothered her, prob-ably because the door was usually closed, its contents out of sight and out of mind.

"How can you look him in the eye after making him wade through your trash like that?" her sister asked. "You ought to be ashamed."

"Well, Caroline, I wasn't expecting a houseguest."

"But don't you keep a guest room?" Caroline seemed be-wildered. "Julia, with all the money you make, you don't even keep a guest room?"

"No," Nina said. "She doesn't."

"He's *staying* in the guest room!" Julia defended the situation. She looked to Lance for support, but he raised both his hands in a gesture of surrender, as if he'd been fighting that fight himself and had decided to leave it to a professional.

"Julia," Caroline asked, "where does Cassie sleep when she stays over?"

"Cassie sleeps with me," Julia said, but kicked herself instantly when Nina chimed, "Well, if it's good enough for Cassie—"

"Nina!" Caroline cut her off. "This is ridiculous; we've got to clean out this room. Today."

Julia turned to Lance, defeated.

Caroline threw open the windows, and soon the fresh, cool breeze began to waft inside and dilute the smell of mothballs. Boxes and bags of junk morphed from unorganized piles into a wave of debris that seemed to swell and resurface every time the bed was hauled from one side of the room to the other. Lance and Nina moved every piece of furniture at least a dozen times, so within an hour, sweat was glistening on his arms and Nina was finding excuses for him to stretch or bend over.

"Can I tell you how nice it is to clean a room that won't be immediately occupied by a five-year-old?" Caroline asked as she scrubbed the hardwood floors with gusto, but Julia barely heard her; she was too busy tearing into boxes and bags like it was Christmas morning. She sifted through the last ten years, finding newspaper clippings of book reviews and old short stories, half-finished afghans and baby blankets, coupons and calendars five years out of date. When most everything was sorted, Julia knew more than half of it was going to have to be thrown away. That was the thought that filled her mind as she stared into a crateful of photos she'd never made time to frame.

"What we need now is bedding," Nina was saying. "Something with color. Something that pops."

"All I need is a place to sleep," Lance said, sounding apologetic.

"Everyone sleeps better in a beautiful bed. It's a scientific fact," Nina said, and Lance cut a look at Julia, who didn't bother trying to explain *science according to Nina*.

After scanning the room, Nina pointed to a flash of color on the top shelf of the closet. "What's that?"

Lance walked to the closet and pulled down an old patchwork quilt that slid into his arms. "It's heavy," he said as Nina helped him pull back the quilted layers to reveal the framed painting it had been protecting.

"This is gorgeous!" Nina exclaimed.

"It's your granny picture!" Caroline rushed toward the old oil painting and examined it like a lost treasure. "Why do you have this hidden up here?"

Julia gazed at the painting that her grandmother had painted of two little girls in the middle of a field. For years, the painting and its twin had hung in her parents' bedroom. But when Caroline married and Julia moved back to the state, Madelyn took the two pieces of art and gave them to her daughters, with strict instructions to give them good homes. It was one of the few things Julia had from her grandmother, and one of the few truly beautiful things she owned.

"Julia," Nina exclaimed. "Why leave something this beautiful crammed in a closet?"

"I'll hang it up eventually," she said. "With the remodeling, I didn't want to risk it getting damaged. When the house is finished, I'll hang it up."

"What do you mean, when you *finish*?" Nina asked. "Have you started?"

"Well, maybe if my decorator hadn't quit—"

"Hey!" Nina jumped to the defensive. "I stuck with you through five types of tile, six cabinet finishes, three professional ranges, seven industrial sinks, two dishwashers, and thirteen cabinet knobs. Do you know how many cabinet knobs are too many? Thirteen. Thirteen is where any self-respecting design professional draws the line."

"Fine," Julia said. "Point taken. Now, can I have my painting back, please?"

"No." Nina pulled it to her chest. "We're using the quilt on the bed, and this is going downstairs. You're going to pick out a place to hang it."

"Nina, I don't think that's—"

"I'm coming back as your decorator for one job only, and this is it."

♣

"What time is it?" Nina asked over the steady pop, pop, pop that was coming from the microwave.

Caroline looked at her watch and answered, "It's half past five."

Nina's eyes flew open and she yelled, "I almost missed *Decorating Derby*!" She jumped off the barstool and ran into the living room, where she grabbed the remote control from Lance's hands and told him, "Scoot over, stud."

"Hey, I was watching . . ." Lance started, but Julia took a seat beside him and said, "Duke loses in overtime."

"How did you know that?" he asked, sincerely impressed.

Julia felt cocky. "ESPN Classic shows old games, or didn't you know?"

"Okay," he said. "Let's watch some decorating."

"Shush up, you two," Nina snapped as she clicked through the channels at breakneck speed, until snappy theme-show music began flooding into the room.

On the screen, Felicia Wallace, the woman who was second in Nina's class at the Wellington Design Academy, was about to begin a major project on a Manhattan brownstone. The designer who had graduated *first* in the class was waiting to be divorced from Jason—again. Julia had to wonder why Nina put herself through the agony of watching a former rival excel on national TV.

"What is this?" Lance asked.

"I'll tell you what *this* is. *This* is the bane of my existence." Nina quickly climbed on her soapbox. "Shows like *Decorating*

*Derby* are convincing the American public that with a gallon of primer and a dozen cardboard toilet-paper rolls, anyone can decorate." She snorted. "Good decorating is like anything else—you get what you pay for."

Caroline came in from the kitchen, a bowl of popcorn in each hand, just in time to see Felicia Wallace introduce the show's official carpenter, Mason Kent. When she glanced at the television, she immediately asked, "Who is *that*?"

"*That* is the worst thing about these shows," Nina declared. "They take a hot guy, strap on a tool belt, and use him to lure thousands of female viewers. This show isn't about design; it's about hot men with power tools. Look at those arms. Look at the way that T-shirt clings to his rippling chest. If you want to do a reality show about decorating, then *at the very least,* your carpenter ought to have jeans that hang below the equator."

Julia picked up on something she hadn't heard from Nina for a very long time. "You *like* him!" she exclaimed. "You've got a *crush* on Mason the hot carpenter guy!"

"I do not." Nina dismissed the suggestion, but a hint of red was appearing on her olive-skinned cheeks.

"I'm a married woman," she insisted. "Well, kind of. I'm a *little bit* married."

Lance glanced down at her hand. "You're not wearing a ring."

"Nina, this is great!" Julia cried. "You have a non-Jason crush. It's a good thing."

"I may be many things," Nina said, "but in love with Felicia's hammer-jockey is not one of them."

"I auditioned to be on one of these shows once," Lance said, grabbing a fistful of popcorn.

"Really?" Julia said, stealing a kernel for herself.

"Yeah," he said. "I used to do a lot of that kind of stuff for my mom, building sets and all. I'm pretty good with my hands."

Nina's elbow was suddenly in Julia's gut. Lance, thankfully, didn't notice.

"It would have been a good gig for me, but I didn't get it. Nina's right, though," he said, filling his mouth with popcorn. "Those guys are actors."

Caroline was glued to the set. "He really knows how to use that sander," she said.

"Caroline!" Julia said, a little surprised at her sister.

"I can't help it." Caroline shrugged. "Every time I ask Steve to do something around the house, he lectures me about comparative advantage and reminds me what an hour of his time bills for at the firm. Do you know how many times I've seen Steve pick up a nail gun, or anything else, for that matter?"

"Do we really want to see Steve with a nail gun?" Nina asked.

"You have a brand-new house, Caroline," Julia said. "You don't need to be married to Mr. Fix-it."

"Well, I wouldn't mind being married to Mr. Knows-how-to-unload-the-dishwasher," Caroline said under her breath.

When Felicia began instructing homeowners on how to wallpaper their den with old newspapers, Nina shifted and dramatically covered her eyes. "Oh, it's too painful. I can't watch anymore. I have to go. Caroline, are you ready?"

"Why? Can't we stay a little longer?"

Julia's jaw dropped. She'd never seen her sister do anything but rush toward her children. Caroline had already spent the better part of a day away from them. She couldn't imagine what force of nature could have brought about such change. Then, she remembered. "So, how's the memoir coming along?"

Caroline rolled her eyes. "Did you know that Ro-Ro had seven different dogs when she was growing up? I do. I even know their names. I know how big they were. I know how she disposed of their bodies when they died."

"I suppose that came in handy," Nina said. "You know, for later."

"Why does this always happen to me?" Caroline cried in disbelief.

"You're a nice person. It comes with the territory," Nina said. "Or so I hear."

Julia asked, "So where is Ro-Ro now?"

"She wants the memoir to include excerpts from her fans. As we speak, she has called an emergency meeting of the Georgias. They're going to put together some notes and get back to me."

"I am so sorry, Caroline," Julia said, meaning it. "Being forced to work with Ro-Ro *and* the Georgias. No one deserves that."

"At least she gave me last night off. Although, technically, I was supposed to use that as an opportunity to scout locations for a series of tasteful black-and-white photos she wants throughout the book. Because, *of course,* I don't have anything else to do." She looked at her sister. "We finally got her settled back at her place, and for once, Steve agreed to stay with the kids. I know they're probably burning the house down even as we speak, but I just can't go back, not yet. She might call there, but she'd never call here."

"Why won't she call here?" Nina asked.

Julia and Caroline said in unison, "It's a long-distance call."

"Ah," Nina said, understanding. "The cheapness pays off."

Caroline added, "Hallelujah."

Just then, the phone rang, and Caroline and Julia looked at each other as if they'd just jinxed themselves and Ro-Ro had invested in nationwide long distance or, Heaven forbid, a cell phone. But Julia checked the caller ID this time, and then picked up. "Hello, mother," she said.

"Julia, it's your mother," Madelyn said, disregarding Julia's greeting. "Your father and I were driving past your house just now, and . . . well . . . you should turn on Channel Two."

Despite Nina's disdain for *Decorating Derby,* she still cried "Hey" when Julia took the remote control and changed the channel to the Tulsa NBC affiliate. Her cries were silenced, however, by the sight of Richard Stone's smirk.

"Who's that?" Caroline asked.

"My agent," Lance said as his heart fell to the pit of his stomach.

All around the little man, spotlights shone through the

early-evening air. Julia leaned closer to the screen, squinting, trying to imagine why the scene looked so familiar. "That's my mailbox!" she yelled. "He's here! He's by the front gate!"

Richard Stone was standing in the glare of spotlights, shielded only by a massive bank of microphones. He squinted into the bright light, then slipped on a pair of reading glasses and cleared his throat. "Ladies and gentlemen," he said as he pulled a piece of paper from the breast pocket of his jacket. "Mr. Collins and Ms. James have prepared a brief statement they would like me to read. I ask that you please hold your questions." He cleared his throat again and began. "Ladies and gentlemen of the press, we ask your understanding and patience as we embark on this, the most important project of our lives. True love, like true art, takes time to perfect and ripen."

"As if I would ever write something with mixed metaphors," Julia scoffed.

Caroline shushed her, and Richard read on.

"We are using this time to let our relationship grow and blossom into the beautiful thing that it will become. We ask your understanding and respect for our privacy during this, a most romantic time." Richard Stone folded the piece of paper and put it away. "I will now be taking questions."

"What are Lance and Julia's future plans?" one reporter yelled.

A smile spread across Richard's face. "They're going to stay here for the time being. Lance has some really sweet offers though, so I expect he'll be getting back to work soon."

"Will Julia go with him?" the reporter followed up.

"Oh." Richard smirked. "I can't imagine keeping the two of them apart."

"He's dead!" Julia yelled and started, full-steam, toward the front door, but Lance grabbed her around the waist and, with the force of her momentum, swung her neatly around with her feet in the air.

"Cool it," he said near her ear, his arms still locked around her.

"Is it true Lance has signed a three-picture deal with Miramax?" a reporter asked.

"I'm afraid I can't comment on that."

"Is it true that Julia's writing a book on wedding planning?"

"Actually," Richard said, "I think Julia's going to be taking some time to support Lance and his career."

Luckily, Lance still had a solid grip on Julia, because she bolted for the door again, and he had to struggle to hold her back. On the television, the questions and the flashes were as bright and loud as ever, but Richard Stone must have decided to quit while he was ahead. "Okay, folks, okay," he said, waving and yelling over the barrage of questions that seemed to be coming from all directions. "That's all I can really say right now. All you need to know is that they're happy, and they're in love, and they're very excited about the baby."

Julia passed out cold.

# Chapter Sixteen

> **WAY #77: Take good care of yourself.**
> If you live alone, then there's no guarantee that someone will be there to take care of you when you're under the weather. So, by all means, take good care of yourself.
>
> —from *101 Ways to Cheat at Solitaire*

Julia opened her eyes and stared overhead, slowly focusing on the water stains and cobwebs that she'd never noticed in the thousands of times she'd walked to her bedroom on the second floor. Other things came into focus, too: a twin mattress; the railing of the stairs; and six legs and six feet, four of which were standing on tiptoes.

"Oh, I wish I'd brought my telescope," Caroline said as she looked through the small, circular window that offered the best view of the county road.

"Did you say 'telescope'?" Lance asked.

"It was Steve's when he was a kid. I keep it in the upstairs playroom so I can keep an eye on Crazy Myrtle."

"Caroline." Julia groaned as she pushed herself upright and fought against her swirling head. "Please tell me you don't really do that!"

Caroline turned to study her recently unconscious sister. "Well, *someone* has to."

"How you doing, sleepyhead?" Lance crouched beside her and asked. Julia felt her face burn red with humiliation. Had she actually fainted? Had Lance carried her up the stairs? *Does he know how much I weigh?*

"Do you need anything?" he asked.

*An untraceable passport and enough cash to get me to Paraguay?*

"No," she muttered.

He turned his attention back to the window, and Julia tried to make the most of the situation. *It's good to know your limits,* she thought, scrolling through a list of all she'd learned since meeting Lance: *Paparazzi attacks equal prison. Fictional babies equal fainting. Now, if I only knew what it would take for me to develop selective amnesia, I'd be set.*

"I've never seen so many lights in my life!" Nina said as she fought with Caroline for position at the window. "I bet every TV crew in the state is camped out there."

Something snapped inside of Julia. Everything came into sharp, clear focus. She jumped up and started down the stairs but stopped suddenly and looked around the landing where they'd been working all afternoon. "Nina, where'd you put that hammer?"

"Julia," Lance soothed as if she were a wild animal. His movements were slow and steady as he slid onto the stair beneath her.

"I am gonna kill that man, Lance!" She looked around once more, then yelled, "Screw the hammer!" and started to push past him.

Unfortunately, it's hard to walk toward vengeance when both your feet are off the floor and the room is suddenly upside down. Julia recognized Lance's terrific rear end staring her in the face. She clawed at his back and kicked, but he didn't let her off his shoulder. He had one arm wrapped around the bend in her knees and the other arm perched way too comfortably on her rear end.

*"Put me down this instant!"*

"Come on, Lance," Julia heard Nina say through the curtain of hair that had fallen over her face. "You don't want to hurt the *baby*."

Julia put her hands on Lance's butt and pushed herself upright enough to face her sister and best friend.

"Nina, this is *so* not funny! People who used to respect me are currently under the impression that I am *shacked* up! And *knocked* up and . . . *many kinds of up!*" Blood rushed to her head. "I don't feel so good," she said, and Lance dropped her onto the mattress.

"Stay there," he ordered, and for once, Julia did exactly as she was told.

"Come on, Julia," Caroline said. "No one is going to believe that about you."

Just then the phone rang. Nina picked it up and looked at the caller ID. "It's Ro-Ro," she said, handing the receiver to Julia, who turned the ringer off. She used the phone to point at her sister.

"Ro-Ro just made a long-distance call, Caroline. Do you still think it's so unbelievable?"

Lance's legs appeared in Julia's peripheral vision. He leaned down and held out a glass of water for her to take. "Thanks," she said, grateful for something to do with her hands. She drank the whole glass before looking back up at him. "And not just for the water," she said sheepishly.

"Oh . . . well." Lance eased down beside her. She felt his weight and sensed his guilt. "Do I have a great agent or what?"

"He is pretty resourceful," Nina added, not helping.

Someone had left the television on downstairs. Julia heard a reporter's voice saying, "Tonight the debate rages on. . . ." and the distant cries of picketers: "Give Lance a chance! Give Lance a chance!" The story continued, but Julia could listen no more.

She stood and gathered her composure. She brushed herself off and said, "I'm going to have to issue a statement. I'll walk down there right now and address them myself. I'll pee on a stick in front of them if that's what it takes, but . . ."

"Julia." Lance stood and held her arms. His voice was cool and steady, with no hint of sarcasm or ridicule, just stability and truth. "The last time you addressed these people, it involved a hard-sided suitcase and a night in jail. I don't really think public urination would be a step up. Do you?" She pondered this, maybe longer than she'd intended, because she felt Lance's grip on her arms tighten. "Julia, you're exhausted. Let's sleep on it. In the morning, we can make a statement or maybe meet with an attorney. But it's getting late. Let's not try to accomplish anything tonight."

Reluctantly, Julia nodded her agreement. "At least there aren't any more pictures. Without pictures, there isn't much fuel for the fire."

Lance smiled, dimples and all, and said, "Exactly."

Halfway down the stairs, Julia hid her face in her hands and yelled, "Oh, what a mess!" Then she decided that if she wasn't going to get to kill Richard Stone with a hammer, she could at least attack the pile of garbage they'd cleaned out of the guest room. She headed to the mountain of boxes and bags, and began hauling them toward the back door, wishing all of life's garbage could disappear so easily. But before she could hurl the first bag into the backyard, Nina grabbed it from her.

"Don't do that!" she exclaimed, clutching the trash bag to her chest. "Don't you watch TV? They'll go through it! They have no pride."

"Nina, I have to do something! This whole night is driving me crazy!"

"Give the trash to me," Caroline said. "Tomorrow's trash day. I'll put everything out with my stuff. And Julia"—she pointed at her sister—"listen to Nina. Until this is over, nothing goes out that door, okay? Not you. Not him. Not even the trash."

Julia whipped off a little salute to her take-no-prisoners sister. "Fine."

"It will be *okay*," Caroline said with a hug. "We'll work it all out tomorrow."

Julia picked up the red eight and tried to find a place for it to go. *Nowhere*. She looked back through the loose cards to the side of the seven stacks and remembered that there had been a black nine in there somewhere. She flipped through the cards until she found it, then she placed it on the red ten and laid the eight down in order. *There. Great. Crisis averted.*

"Now that's cheating," Lance said from the doorway of her bedroom.

Julia was taken aback by the thought of him watching her nightly insomnia ritual. "I'm good at cheating," she said, growing defensive. "Cheating is what I do."

He grinned. "You should write a book."

"Maybe I'll do that," she said and smiled despite her best efforts otherwise. She thought that might put an end to the conversation, but instead he crossed his arms and asked softly, "Are you okay, Julia? You had me scared for a minute there."

Suddenly, Julia wasn't sitting on her bed playing solitaire;

she was standing on a busy street, feeling the rain in the wind as Lance Collins stood behind her; she was in a taxi, rolling down the window, offering him a ride. Seeds planted that day at Stella's were growing wild, out of control, and far beyond her normal borders. She stared back down at the cards, searching for her next move. But instead of finding a way to change the cards to suit her situation, Julia found herself saying, "If I can't stop Richard Stone, I'll lose everything." It was something that until then, she hadn't even admitted to herself.

"No you won't," Lance said simply. "But we'll stop it anyway." As he turned to leave, he looked back at her and said, "You should try milk and honey."

"Excuse me?"

"To help you sleep." He stepped closer. "My mom's an insomniac, too, but when she's up, she doesn't like to be alone, so I'd keep her company. I was the only kid in the fourth grade who operated on less than three hours of sleep a night. But I was also the only ten-year-old who knew all the Shakespearean soliloquies, so it was probably a pretty fair trade. Plus"—he cocked his head—"I could build stuff. Anyway, she always drank milk and honey. It helped."

As she watched Lance, she realized that part of him was still that little boy, acting his way through the night to entertain his tired mother.

"You should call her," Julia said finally. "If she's like me, she's up. You should let her know what's going on."

He nodded, then slipped his hand under his T-shirt to

scratch his chest. "I'll go do that," he said. Then he reached down and massaged the base of Julia's neck with one hand while he leaned over her, studying her cards. It felt too darn wonderful to make him stop. "You're under too much stress," he said and headed for the door. At the threshold, he stopped and turned toward her. "I'll bring you some warm milk, if you want."

"Whole milk?" she questioned.

"What other kind is there?"

# Chapter Seventeen

"Hey," Caroline said early the next morning when she called Julia on her cell phone. "Why don't you guys come over?"

"It's Ro-Ro, isn't it?" Julia asked. "You finally snapped, and now you need my brains and Lance's muscles to help you dispose of the body."

"Very funny," Caroline quipped. "No, actually, I . . . why don't you come over?"

"Caroline, there are reporters staking out my property. I can't exactly go cruising around the countryside with a hot man."

"So you admit he's hot?" Caroline exclaimed.

"No. I mean hot as in stolen, as in I'm not supposed to

have him. One more picture of us together and my career is over, or have you forgotten?"

"I thought you'd say that, so I called Nina," Caroline stated. "She's got a plan."

♦

Lance looked out the back window at Nina's VW and said, "You've got to be kidding me." Then he looked at Nina in her tightly belted trench coat, floppy hat, and dark glasses, and realized just how serious she probably was.

"It won't be for long," Nina said. "We can let you out as soon as we ditch them."

"Ditch them?" Lance exclaimed. "These are professional paparazzi! They're not exactly easy to ditch."

"My father was a used-car dealer in Oklahoma," Nina said, ripping off her Jackie O shades as if her virtue had been questioned. "I've been driving since I was twelve years old. I assure you, *I* can ditch anyone."

"Nina," Julia said, looking at the tiny trunk that her best friend had just suggested Lance crawl into. "Don't all interior decorators own vans?"

"Julia, the van is for company business only. This," Nina said, gesturing up and down at Lance, "is personal."

"Okay," Julia conceded, "then we'll take my car."

"Um," Lance interjected. "Believe me, no one is a bigger fan of finding another vehicle than I am, but your car is in front of the house. I can't go out the front door. And you can't exactly pull around here without making it look like something's up."

Julia thought about her driveway, which was almost a half mile long and full of twists and turns. Normal people could barely see her house from the road, but the vultures that were camped in the ditches weren't exactly normal. "Fine then," Julia said. "We just won't go."

"Jules," Nina said, "we've got to go."

"Why?"

Nina didn't answer. She shifted her gaze between Lance and Julia and bit her lip, weighing some unspecified options.

"*Nina . . .* " Julia said, a threat in her voice.

"Caroline wouldn't say!" Nina blurted. "She just said that I had to get both of you to her house and not to waste a minute about it. So, see, we've got to go!"

Julia turned and started upstairs. "I'm going to go get blankets. Lance can lay down in the backseat. We'll cover him up." She looked at Lance. "Is that okay with you?"

He nodded. "That's fine."

♠

Twenty dirt roads, nine illegal U-turns, and one mad dash in front of a train later, Nina turned into Caroline's seemingly uninhabited development.

*My very own bat cave,* Julia mused as Nina pulled into the garage space where Steve parked his Camry on the rare occasions when he was actually home. Caroline hit the button and the door started down, blocking out the sunlight, proving it was safe to pull Lance from beneath the pile of blankets. One look at him made Julia wonder who had had the worst of it—Julia, who could see the road, or Lance, whose trip was left up to the imagination.

"Okay, Caroline, I'm here. Spill it," Julia said.

But Caroline obviously didn't share Julia's sense of urgency. Instead, she led her guests into the kitchen and asked, "Can I get anyone a drink? Some fruit? Juice maybe?"

"I don't want juice, Caroline," Julia snapped. "I want to know what the . . ." her voice trailed off as she noticed Nina, who had taken off her hat and was slipping out of her trench coat, revealing her brand-new GIVE LANCE A CHANCE T-shirt.

"*Nina!*" Julia cried.

Nina looked down at her shirt as if she'd forgotten what she was wearing. A broad grin stretched across her face. "I got you one, too."

"Nina, this is *so* not—"

"Julia, I took the wrong box!" Caroline cried, the words exploding from her lips. Every eye turned toward Caroline, who looked down at her hands, spinning the wedding band on her finger.

Julia looked around and asked, "What box? *What* are you talking about?"

"Yesterday. The junk we cleaned out of Lance's room."

"*Lance's* room?!" Julia questioned.

"—one of the boxes was old manuscripts. I took it by mistake. I'm sorry."

Julia exhaled. She hadn't known she'd been holding her breath. She eased onto a barstool as the tension slipped away and she realized her sister's "crime" had been minor.

Then, worry was replaced by annoyance. "We had to sneak over here because you wanted to give me my box back?"

"No," Caroline hurried to say. "Steve put it out with the trash this morning."

"Oh," Julia said, surprised. An odd sense of grief came over her as she realized what that meant. "Everything I ever wrote was in that box. Short stories, essays, drafts of my books." The weight of loss settled down on her. "Now they're gone. . . ."

Caroline eased onto a stool beside her sister. She pulled Julia's hand into her own and patted it. "That's the problem. They're not exactly *gone*."

Lance said, "Maybe it's vertigo from the car ride talking, but you've lost me."

"We all know that Myrtle's crazy," Caroline said slowly. "She wears a housecoat all day long, and she drinks in the mornings, and . . . she likes to go through the trash. Julia, honey, I saw her take your box."

"Oh, no!"

Lance had heard about spontaneous combustion, but until that moment, he didn't believe it was really possible. Julia flew out of the kitchen, her long, red hair waving behind her like flames. She reached the family room, then turned and began to hyperventilate. She kept yelling, "Oh, no! Oh, no! *Oh, no!*"

and waving her hands in front of her face as if trying to make her fingernails dry was a matter of life and death.

Caroline and Nina stood by, looking as useless as Lance felt. Finally, he stepped closer to Julia and said, "So she's got early drafts of your books. What's she gonna do, sell them on eBay?"

"*Oh my god!*" Julia yelled. Lance seriously thought she was going to pass out. He couldn't believe he'd actually made things worse.

"There are more than Julia James manuscripts in that box," Caroline said as she rubbed her sister's back while Julia sat on an ottoman, holding her head between her knees, trying to slow her breathing.

"There are Veronicas in that box?" Nina yelled, amazed, finally catching on to what Lance was missing. "You didn't burn the Veronicas?"

Julia's head popped up. The color had drained from her face, and crazy, static-empowered hairs circled around her head. "Not the first one." She sniffed. "It was the first thing I ever got published—ever. When *Table for One* made the best-seller lists, I knew there could be a scandal, but I couldn't . . . I should have, I know. And now . . ."

Her head disappeared between her knees again, and Caroline kept rubbing her back in slow circles. Caroline was patient as she explained. "When Julia first moved to New York, she wasn't making very much money, and you know how proud she is. She wasn't going to ask for help so . . . well, for a while she was a . . ." Her voice trailed off. Lance expected her to say stripper or telemarketer, but then Julia straightened and finished.

"Romance novelist."

"She could write at night and still work in the industry during the day," Caroline explained. "She used a pen name. The three of us are the only people in the whole state who know about it. Not even Mom and Dad know."

"*Especially* not Mom and Dad." Julia's voice came from between her knees.

"And the IRS," Caroline added, ever the tax attorney's wife. "Of course the IRS knew."

"Well, that's about to change," Nina said. "Crazy Myrtle is about to go pilfering through that box, and it won't take her long to figure it out."

The four of them stared at one another. Then Nina said, "We have to get it back. We've got to break in." Then she continued: "Lance is a man. He can help"—setting the women's movement back twenty-five years, at least to the days before *Charlie's Angels.*

"Nina, that's ridiculous," Caroline said.

"I told you," Nina said, as if she was holding a surefire answer to their prayers and Caroline was refusing to listen. *"Lance can help."*

"Whoa," Lance said. "I'm not committing any felonies until I see for myself exactly why the world will end if I don't help you three."

Caroline disappeared. When she came back, she was carrying

a handful of worn paperbacks. "Here." She handed a book to Lance, and he took it. "That's the first one. That's the one Myrtle's got."

Lance looked at the small block of paper in his hands. It had a bright cover with a half-naked man and a bosomy woman in a tight embrace. He read the title: "*Tomorrow's Temptation* by Veronica White." Then he looked down at the straightlaced woman he'd come to know. "Hello, Veronica," he teased.

"Hey, category romance is *big business*," she said defensively. "I wasn't going into the slush pile. I was going to get published and get paid." She crossed her arms over her chest and raised her chin. "It was all about the math."

"Sure," Lance said, not trying to hide his doubts. "This looks very mathematical."

"I'll have you know that the majority of all popular fiction sales are in the romance genre, not to mention more than half of all the paperbacks," Julia stated. "There are over fifty million readers in North America alone!"

"Okay," Lance shot back. "So it's big business and you were good at it. *Then what's the big deal?*" he asked.

"The 'big deal,'" Julia said, "is that Veronica White sold something that Julia James tells women they don't need. *This*"—she snatched the book from his hands—"plus *you*"—she used the book to hit his shoulder—"equals *hypocrite*," she gestured to herself. Then she dropped into a chair and laid one arm dramatically over her eyes. Lance thought she looked like Juliet right after she swallowed the poison.

Lance walked to the remaining pile of books and selected one. He studied the paperback novel in his hands and said, "Veronica White. You made that up?"

"Yes," Caroline answered.

He turned to the back cover of the book and studied the black-and-white photograph of a timeless, ageless woman wearing a black turtleneck with stark black hair pulled tightly away from a classic face. If she hadn't been on the back of a book, he might have expected to find her on an ancient coin. "Who's the babe?"

"The babe"—Caroline laughed—"is Ro-Ro."

"*No,*" he said, disbelieving.

Caroline took the paperback from him and studied it like a person staring at a family heirloom. "It's an old picture, taken when she was between husbands and going through a Bohemian phase."

Lance looked between the book and the woman who had written it. He saw the same strong features, the same graceful presence; the picture might have been of Ro-Ro, but the image, Lance decided, was all Julia. Then he remembered the dour old woman the graceful girl in the photo had become. What a waste.

Caroline went on. "We didn't think anyone would ever figure it out. When we found the picture, it looked so modern and she was so beautiful in it that *we* didn't even know it was her until she told us."

"So does she know?" Lance asked.

"Good gracious, no," Caroline said. "I can just see Miss Sycamore Hills putting her face on the back of a book. There'd be hell to pay."

"Are you kidding?" Nina asked. "She would love it."

"Deep down maybe," Caroline conceded.

"Deep down definitely," Nina said.

"No deep down about it," Julia said, sounding more confident than her sister and best friend combined. "She'd love it, and she'd *blab*."

They sat in silence for a long time, each of them trying to find a magic solution, a time machine, an error-proof plan. After a while, Julia straightened and said, "Why am I panicking? I'll just go ask for it back. I'll offer to pay her if that's what it takes." She stood and began looking for her purse. "I don't know how much cash I've got, but—"

"Julia, that won't work," Caroline said, sounding grim.

Julia looked at her sister. "Do you have a better idea?"

"No, but I can promise you that knocking on the door isn't the way to go. Steve tried talking to her, remember? The woman is a few dishes shy of a load. Right now, she thinks it's just our trash. I can't imagine what she'd do if she knew it was something we really wanted."

Silence came again. Lance tried to remember his life before crawling into that cab with Julia, but he couldn't. His apartment, his friends, they all seemed like a long-forgotten dream. He looked at Julia, the woman who had made a name and a life for herself by telling the world that romance wasn't the requisite for happiness, and he remembered that it had taken just one scandalous lie to throw her whole world out of balance. Lance didn't want to imagine the power of a juicy piece of truth.

Nina said, "We could break in," as if, in the silence, her idea would fall on more favorable ears.

"No," Lance said, and Nina let it drop.

"I've got it," Caroline said, a lightbulb shining brightly above her head. "We could say it's a book you brought home to edit, and it got mixed in with some of your stuff. Doesn't mean you wrote it. It's a mistake," she finished.

Julia was shaking her head. "It's going to have my name and address at the top of the cover sheet and my handwritten notes all over the text. It's covered with my fingerprints—literally and figuratively." She took a deep breath and added, "That's the bad news. The good news is that the Veronica is at the bottom of the box. With any luck, we've got some time."

♣

*Do you ever get too old or successful to hide in the bathroom?* Julia wondered as she sat on the toilet lid of what Caroline liked to call "the pool bath." Of course, Steve and Caroline didn't have a pool, but they had the bathroom for one—just in case—a fact that had seemed ridiculous to Julia until she went searching for someplace far away from the noise of the vacuum cleaner and the *Dora the Explorer* videos.

Staring at her reflection in the mirror, Julia saw past and

future collide. She got up and leaned into the light, wanting to make sure her eyes weren't playing tricks on her, but nope, there it was, a zit right next to a wrinkle.

*This is officially the worst day of my life.*

Julia's cell phone lay beside the sink, but it felt a hundred miles away. She stared at it longingly, daring herself to pick it up and dial. She knew the number by heart. She had free long distance. She wasn't in roam. Really, there wasn't a reason in the world to keep putting it off, but the phone lay on the counter like nuclear waste, and Julia stared at it, as if expecting it to sprout legs and scamper off and make her decision for her.

She leaned closer to the mirror, tilted her head, and practiced what she'd say. "Hi, Abby, it's Julia James. . . ."

*No good,* Julia thought. She straightened her back and tried again, this time aiming for "time-crunched-career-gal."

"Abby, Julia James here."

*No, I have to sound nice,* she reminded herself, so she smiled, turned up her accent, and did her best version of "everyone's favorite girl from Oklahoma."

"Hi, Ms. Warner, this is Julia James. Could I have a minute of your time?"

Still, the greeting didn't convey the sense of urgency that Julia felt. She gripped the stone countertop, squinted her eyes, and sunk into "desperate, almost-middle-aged has-been."

"Candon Jeffries screwed me over. Wanna make him pay?"

Julia stopped for a second to ponder whether or not she was doing the right thing. It might be easier on her mind and her ego just to jump ship, take her future books to any of Eli-Winter's rivals. But, like it or not, her first three books already belonged to them, and she didn't feel like leaving her firstborn behind. Still, she knew the only way she could bring herself to stay with Eli-Winter was if Abby Warner was on her side. Abby was the grande dame of nonfiction, the woman with nine of the top ten bestsellers of all time to her credit, the person with the power to crush Candon like a bug—assuming she wanted to. No one gets as successful as Abby Warner without knowing the power of a buck, and Julia knew that however much it pained her, the "Lance Collins situation" had been very good for business.

So she took a deep breath, picked up her cellular phone, eased herself down on the closed lid of the toilet, and dialed her publisher's main phone number. A switchboard operator came on the line, and Julia asked to speak to Abby Warner.

"I'm sorry," a well-trained male secretary said once she'd been transferred. "Ms. Warner isn't available at the moment." Julia was fluent in the language of the publishing industry, and knew this translated to "Go away, loser, we don't accept unsolicited trash."

*It's now or never,* Julia thought, holding her breath. "Will you see if she's available for Julia James?"

A pause from New York City. Then the man asked, "Miss James?"

"Yes," Julia said. "I'll hold."

It seemed like a lifetime as she waited. A dozen horrific scenarios ran through her mind, the worst of which consisted of her being transferred to Candon and told that she shouldn't forget whose author she really was. What if Abby Warner hated her books? What if Abby Warner hated her? What if the most influential woman in modern publishing thought she was a hack, a wash-up, a dud?

Then Abby came on the line. "Sweetheart, are you okay?" The woman gave her no time to answer before she jumped in again. "Everybody's talking about it. Now why don't you tell me what's *really* going on?"

"It's not true, Abby. None of it."

"Oh, honey. I can't tell you what a relief that is."

"It is?" Julia asked, amazed that Abby was seeing her side of it. "Candon was thrilled. Sales are through the roof—"

"Candon wouldn't know integrity if it bit him on his ass. So I guess you want to come over to me," Abby said, but before Julia could answer, the editor blew right past her. "Of course I want you! Consider it done. And what's this I hear about a baby?"

"Completely untrue."

"Listen, Jules," Abby said. Very few people called Julia "Jules," but she made the split-second decision that if Abby Warner wanted to be one of them, all the better. "What's this agent's name, the one whose face is in front of all the cameras?"

"Richard Stone."

"Don't worry about this jerk. We've got people who dispose of men like him for a living."

Julia didn't want to think what "dispose of" might mean

to the woman who'd edited an international bestseller on the top secrets of the Mob.

"Oh, Abby, that sounds great. But I'm afraid the blood's already in the water. I've got photographers camped outside my house. They're not going to give up just because Richard Stone goes away."

"Sure they are," Abby said. "I have it on good authority there's a supermodel with a bun in the oven even though her billionaire sugar daddy had a vasectomy six years ago. You're about to be old news."

Julia breathed a sigh of relief. "Oh, Abby, that's wonderful."

"Great! Jules, I get the feeling there's something here you're not telling me."

Actually, there were a lot of things Julia hadn't told her simply because Abby hadn't allowed her time to speak. She thought about Crazy Myrtle, the fact that Lance was living with her, and the missing Veronica, and she also remembered what her mother always said about lasting relationships being rooted in truth. She adjusted her grip on the phone and aimed for "completely reliable business associate."

"No," Julia said. "Nothing else."

# Chapter Eighteen

> **WAY #18: Value persistence.**
> The single people who cope best with life are those who are persistent and surround themselves with people who don't settle for second best. People who are truly happy set their sights on their goals and then keep plugging away until they reach them.
>
> —from *101 Ways to Cheat at Solitaire*

"Grandpa calls him Twirp," Cassie was saying. "That means small, contemptible person," she explained to Lance as Julia eased down the hall toward the nursery. She could see Nick sleeping peacefully in his crib and Lance standing beside him with Cassie mounted firmly on his back. "At first, I didn't want a little brother," Cassie went on. "But I know women have longer life expectancies, so it's okay that I'm older."

"Five going on forty, huh?" Lance said softly as Julia appeared in the doorway.

"Oh, yeah," she whispered back. She took Cassie from Lance and felt the little girl's arms and legs wrap around her. "Whatcha doing, girlie?" she asked her niece.

"I'm explaining how to be a sister, because Lance doesn't have one."

"Oh?" Julia asked, eyebrows raised. "That's very nice of you."

Julia carried Cassie toward the door. She felt Lance place his hand on the small of her back and guide her around the array of toys that Cassie had left, like a trail of breadcrumbs, to follow. *Don't we look like a little family,* Julia thought, but she didn't protest as they eased down the long hall.

"Lance knows Shrek!" Cassie squealed.

Julia cut him an inquiring look.

"Well," he fudged, "I know a guy who works as Mike Myers's stand-in."

For Cassie, and by extension Julia, that was close enough.

"There you are!" Caroline shouted as she suddenly appeared at the top of the stairs. She leaned over and fought to catch her breath. "I ought to be a size two, as many times a day as I go up and down these things," she said to no one but herself. Then she straightened, looked at Lance and Julia, and exclaimed, "His agent is here!"

Instinctively, Julia tightened her grip on Cassie, as if she were going to have to get the children to safety before the shots started to fly.

"You didn't let him in, did you?" Lance asked.

"No," Nina said, appearing behind Caroline. "He's at Myrtle's."

♥

Caroline hadn't been exaggerating when she said she could stand in the upstairs playroom and keep an eye on Crazy Myrtle. As Julia peered through the telescope, she could see straight into what must be Myrtle's formal living room, where Richard Stone sat with the older woman, enjoying a cup of tea. At least Julia thought it was tea. It could just as easily have been human blood.

"Oh, she's enjoying this," Caroline said, sounding bitter. When a buzzer sounded from deep within the house, she bolted for the stairs. "Whites are done."

"Caroline," Julia said, "can't that *wait*?"

Caroline wheeled. "Julia, the sun is going to come up tomorrow, whether my family has clean underwear or not." She took a step down the stairs. "I'll be right back."

With Caroline gone, Lance was next in turn for the telescope. "How's Harvey?" he asked, and Julia had to remind herself that Lance had never even met Harvey; she fought to remember that only a few days before, she had never met Lance.

"He's better," Julia said, reflecting on the quick call she'd shared with Francesca after she'd said good-bye to Abby. "He'll be in rehab for a while, but things look good."

"Great," Caroline said over the heaping pile of sheets and towels she had dropped in the center of the playroom floor.

"Mom will be glad to hear African violets haven't lost their healing power."

Caroline plopped down on the floor and started folding like a pro. Lance joined her, and Nina shifted into place for telescope duty. Julia watched Lance with the laundry. As he neatly tucked the corners of a fitted sheet into one another, she thought, *He actually knows what he's doing.* "You really didn't have a sister?" she asked.

He grinned. "I bake, too."

"So what did your new editor say when you told her about the lost Veronica?" Caroline asked as she segued from sheets to hand towels.

"Well . . ." Julia started.

"You didn't tell her," Caroline said, sounding completely unsurprised. "Julia, you're going into business with her. She's taking a chance on you. You can't let—"

"She doesn't need to know. Abby Warner is used to dealing with the nonfiction big boys—corporate CEOs, prime ministers, chairmen of the Joint Chiefs of Staff. Trust me, she's not going to give someone with Veronica White's sales history the time of day."

"If you say so," Caroline chimed.

"Maybe we're reading too much into this," Lance said. "Richard Stone's not going to care what type of books you used to write."

"Are you kidding?" Julia asked. "This is fresh wood for the fire. This keeps the headlines on the front page a few days longer." She looked out the window at Myrtle's house and the decaying subdivision and fought not to say, *This is how my career might end*.

"What happens when he *reads* it?" Nina added sheepishly.

Caroline's hand flew to her mouth. "He's going to notice."

"I noticed as soon as I saw the picture," Nina agreed. "Lance fits the description exactly. That's why I thought it was true!"

"What aren't you telling me?" Lance demanded.

Caroline and Nina stared at each other, then Nina gave Caroline a "go ahead" nod, and Caroline said, "It's about you."

"Caroline!" Julia cried.

But Nina picked up the novel and began to read over Julia's protests: "Philippe's arms, still sore from the long journey, hung loosely by his side while the wind blew through his *dark brown hair*. His *gray eyes* squinted against the rising sun. His *chin* . . ."

"So, there are some similarities," Julia jumped in, stopping Nina.

"*Similarities?*" Nina turned to Lance, thrusting the book into his hands. "The hero looks like you. *Exactly* like you. Twelve years ago, Julia wrote a romance novel about a man who looks like you," Nina finished. Then, keeping the same tone she'd had before, she said, "I'm hungry," and she and her GIVE LANCE A CHANCE T-shirt disappeared down the stairs.

Lance looked at the book again. "How many of these did you write?" he asked.

Julia answered, "Eight."

He studied her, then asked, "Did they sell well?"

She had to laugh a little. "Yeah," she said. "They did *really* well."

"There's nothing wrong with what you wrote," he said. "There's nothing wrong with who you are."

"I'm not her," Julia stated.

"Yes, you are. Isn't that what this crisis is about? And what I'm telling you is that there's no shame in that."

She struggled to believe Lance, but she knew too well that the world wasn't that idyllic. Veronica White died the day Candon Jeffries took Julia to lunch at the Ritz. A card turned over. Everything changed. She had traded one life for another, and to be the person she was *now,* no one could ever know who she'd been *then.* "No one can know about these books," she said simply and solidly, steadying herself for the arguments that would come next. But she felt Lance's hand on her arm and knew the topic was closed.

"Something's happening," Caroline spoke from the telescope. A moment passed while Lance and Julia crowded around. "Yep. There he goes."

Together, they watched Myrtle's front door open and Richard step onto the front porch. He shook the woman's hand and turned to leave, walking with a slight bounce in his step through the underdeveloped area between the unfinished houses across the street.

Lance eased away from the window. "Crazy Myrtle doesn't

know what she's got yet. Or, if she does, she's smart enough not to share it with Stone, and hold out for someone bigger. And *he* certainly doesn't know what she's got."

"How do you know that?" Julia asked.

"Because he wasn't carrying anything. If that manuscript is what you say it is, no way in hell does Richard Stone walk out without it."

"We could steal it," Nina said from the doorway. She was eating a cherry Popsicle, and the juice ran, like blood, down her hands. It made for an ominous scene.

In unison, they all yelled "No!"

# Chapter Nineteen

The fire crackled, and her house felt warm. Julia stretched her legs across the couch, trying to focus on a back issue of *Publishers Weekly,* but she kept looking down at Lance, who lay on the floor beneath her with his feet near the fireplace, reading Veronica White's first book. Either he was a very slow reader or he was very thorough. *Slow. Definitely slow. Nothing there to savor,* she said to herself, the way a highway patrolman says "Nothing to see here, folks." Yet that didn't change the fact that a man was lying on the floor, reading her deepest secret, literally. To make matters worse, every few pages he'd moan.

He turned slightly, rested his elbow on the floor and his head in the palm of his upturned hand, and read aloud: "Isabella's hands, small and narrow but fiercely strong, gripped the horse's reins as if she were holding on to life itself. Her blood ran hot beneath her cool, pale skin, and the pounding of her heart matched the pounding of the horse's hooves. . . ."

He climbed onto his knees and inched closer, putting his elbows on the couch beside her, crowding into Julia's space. He read on: "Isabella's mind outran the Thoroughbred as she leapt in space and time between her desperate flight on the runaway stallion and the strange figure she had seen the night before, the silhouette that seemed to call to her, a ghost from another lifetime."

"You're an excellent reader," Julia said dryly as she tried to snatch the book away, but he was too quick and too strong. In a flash, he was on the edge of the couch, with Julia pinned to the cushions behind him. One large hand was pressing against her collarbone while the other held the book far away from her flailing arms. Heat burned from his fingers through her T-shirt, and he continued to read, despite her constant jabs and lunges. He read louder, drowning out the sound of Julia's cries.

"The mud-soaked road didn't slow the stallion's hooves."

"Lance, *give me the* . . ."

"Her thin nightgown flew violently in the night wind, her unruly auburn hair as wild as the horse's mane."

"*I want that* . . ."

Lance brought the book to her lips, silencing her. "Just how thin was that nightgown?" he whispered.

She stammered. Lance laughed out loud. She gasped and struggled harder, but Lance lifted the book and continued to read.

"A bolt of lighting stretched across the sky," he exclaimed as if he himself had been struck with electricity. "The horse leapt from the road, chasing the thunder, and before Isabella knew what was happening, she and the horse were gone, as if transported to another world."

"Very nice, Lance," Julia said, finally prying his hand from her and straightening herself on the couch. She turned and planted her feet on the floor beside him. "You get an A-plus. Now you can stop."

She tried to stand, but he wrapped his arm around her waist and pulled her nearly into his lap. "Wait." Both arms were around her then, squeezing her tight. "This is my favorite part," he whispered near her ear and read on.

"The man in whose arms she lay seemed half angel and half demon, too strong and brave to be a mortal man. She looked up into his hard, gray eyes and felt herself shudder. He held her in strong arms that seeped warmth through her thin gown and brought her another, deeper kind of runaway emotion."

Lance lowered the book and shifted her effortlessly against the arm of the couch. He stared into her with those same eyes, smiled with that same mouth, and said, "I like your stuff, Veronica."

He held her there a moment too long. Then he shifted, and

she felt his weight pressing down on her and realized how warm and soft a hard, strong man could be. "Tell me, Ms. White, where do you get your ideas?"

"That's it!" Julia snapped, lunging for and grabbing the book, but she found herself sprawled across him.

Lance twisted, trapping her beneath him on the couch.

"What would Isabella have done there?"

"Let me go!" she cried, but the harder Julia fought to regain control of the situation, the wider Lance smiled.

"This is a pretty good workout," he said. "You're cute when you're scrappy."

Her hair was as wild as the rest of her, and Julia literally couldn't see straight. She lay, tangled in a web of arms and legs, and said, "You are enjoying this way too much!"

"You started it, Veronica."

"Don't call me that!"

They scrambled and tumbled to the floor, and as soon as Julia was able to right herself, she grabbed the book and scampered behind the sofa, using it as a barricade between them. "Hey," Lance said. "I was reading that." He climbed onto the sofa, so she stepped back, toward the kitchen, farther from his reach.

"I know you were reading," she said. "I *heard* you."

Then, with more agility than Julia thought humanly possible, Lance sprang over the back of the sofa and plucked the book out of her hands. As he walked past her to his old place on the floor, he used the book to slap her on the butt. She jumped, but he nonchalantly sunk to the floor and continued to read by firelight. After a long while, she saw a smirk rise on his lips, and without looking at her, he said, "You are very talented, Veronica."

Julia couldn't get to her cell phone fast enough. "Get your night-vision goggles ready," she said when Nina answered. "We're going in."

# Chapter Twenty

> **WAY #33: Utilize professional resources for professional tasks.**
> Being independent and happily single doesn't mean you have to do everything yourself; always know what is better left in the hands of a professional. And if you *do* decide to tackle your own project, take the time to research the task and acquire the tools that will enable you to work like a pro.
> —from *101 Ways to Cheat at Solitaire*

"I'm the lookout," Caroline said with more cheer than should ever belong in that sentence. It made Julia wonder if the James sisters, like the James brothers, had been cut out for a life of crime. The answer was obvious—no, probably not. Then she noticed the walkie-talkie that Caroline had duct-taped to her shoulder, and Julia reconsidered, deciding that there might be a little bandit blood in them after all. Steve was out of town on business, her daughter was asleep downstairs, her infant son dozed in the corner of the room, and Caroline was about to do the craziest thing she'd done, maybe in her entire life. Julia studied her sister's face and realized it looked good on her.

"But how are we getting in?" Lance asked for the hundredth time.

Nina dismissed him. "I said I took care of that."

"*How?*" Lance demanded, and Julia knew he wouldn't budge from that room until someone, evidently Nina, had laid out the plan in detail.

"She has these old tapestries," Nina said. "Some of them are pretty valuable. She's called every design firm in town, wanting to sell them, so today I went by to give her an estimate. But what I was really doing was checking out the joint." Proudly, Nina tapped the notebook in front of her. "When her back was turned, I unlocked a window." She finished by raising her eyebrows a few times in quick succession.

Julia looked between Caroline and Nina and made a mental note that it might be time to make new friends. *I just hope I won't be doing it in prison.*

"Fine," Lance said. "There's an open window. What else do we know?"

"I told her that the tapestries were valuable and asked how she had them protected. She didn't mention a security system."

Julia recognized the squeamish look on Nina's face. "What *did* she mention?"

It took a sharp pinch to the fleshy part of Nina's arm to make her say "pit bull."

"She doesn't have a dog," Caroline scoffed. "I've been watching that house for months and I've never seen a dog."

"Exactly," Nina said, point proven. "That's why I didn't bring it up."

Caroline moved a box of wet wipes from the changing table and unrolled a set of detailed diagrams of the four house styles allowed in the development. She pulled out the floor plan for the smallest of the possible houses, the one the bankrupt contractor had chosen to build for his mother. It showed that the window Nina had unlocked was in the rear of the house, the "keeping room."

"Okay," Caroline said as everyone gathered around. "I'm going to stay here and be central control." She used a turkey baster to point to the diagram as she carried on. "I can only see into the formal living room, formal dining room, keeping room, and part of the kitchen. But I can keep an eye out for lights coming on and movement in the south side of the house. We have emergency exits here and here." She placed Candy Land game pieces on top of the locations of the pedestrian door in the garage and the French doors off the patio. "Take this." She handed Nina the other walkie-talkie. "If you see anything strange, radio back to base, and I'll tell you whether or not to abort."

*Abort? Emergency exits? Central control? What's next,* Julia wondered, *code names and tubes of lipstick that double as rocket launchers?*

Undaunted, Caroline carried on. "Nick wakes up to eat

most nights about one-thirty. I've never noticed any activity over there then, and judging from the number of whiskey bottles Myrtle hauls to the curb on recycling days, I think that's as good a time as any to go in." She paused to survey the troops. "Does that sound okay?" she asked. There were nods all around, so Caroline finished. "Until then, we should consider ourselves in a holding pattern."

Surprisingly, Julia found herself starting to relax. *We've got a plan,* she thought as she, Nina, and Lance shared "this might actually work" glances in the playroom. A feeling of cockiness was starting to build when the doorbell rang and, despite their cool bravado, all four of them nearly jumped through the roof.

"What's with the getups?" Jason asked, looking at Julia, Nina, and Caroline, who stood in the foyer, decked out in black. "You look like rejects from mime academy."

"We're going clubbing," Nina coolly lied, ever the used-car saleman's daughter.

"You three?" Jason asked, eyebrows raised.

"Yep," Caroline agreed. "We're gonna pick up guys."

Caroline had forgotten that she had the walkie-talkie taped to her shirt. Julia jumped and tried to stand in front of her, but Jason had already noticed and said, "What's that?"

"Baby monitor," Julia said.

"Why is it taped to you?" Jason asked.

"Babies are a lot of work, Jason," Julia snapped. "Families are a lot of work. But you know that already. Isn't that why you told Nina you never want to have kids?"

Nina looked troubled, but Jason was unfazed.

He just smirked and pointed to the walkie-talkie. "Won't that get in the way of picking up guys?"

"Not really." Lance's voice carried down the staircase. "I'm already here."

Lance strolled toward the door, looking strong and territorial. Julia thought her heart was going to pound out of her chest as a thought settled firmly in her mind: *I actually know a man like this*. He stopped ten feet from Jason, and Julia realized how Lance had survived as a kid, moving from town to town, living without a father. He was a good man and a great actor, and at that moment, he was acting like someone who would dearly love to beat the crap out of Jason.

Testosterone bounced off the marble floors of the foyer as the two men sized each other up.

"Justin, isn't it?"

"Jason."

"Oh, right. What brings you by?" Lance asked.

"I'm looking for Tiny here," Jason said, and snapped his fingers in an annoying gesture that Julia had seen him do ever since the seventh grade. "Got a couple of movie tickets. Thought she'd want to go."

"Really?" Lance said. "What are you gonna see?"

Jason waved the question away. "It doesn't really—"

Lance cut him off. "If you're asking the lady to a movie because you've got an extra ticket, you ought to tell her what the movie is. So, Jason, what movie is it?"

Julia's eyes darted back and forth, trying to understand this strange phenomenon; the bully was being bullied.

"I need to see my wife. Nina, grab your purse," Jason said, taking her arm and starting toward the door. "Let's go for a drive."

"Hey," she cried. "Stop it."

Lance stepped toward the door, blocking Jason's path of escape, but Jason still had a firm grip on Nina's thin arm.

Julia stepped forward. "Nina and I have plans tonight, Jason."

Jason turned on her, twenty years' worth of anger seeping into his voice. "Maybe Nina doesn't want to be your date tonight! Huh? Did you ever think of that, Julia? Tiny's got a man; she doesn't need to compensate for you not having one."

"Don't call me Tiny," Nina said, sounding clearer and stronger than she'd sounded in Jason's presence in years. "I hate it!" She cringed. "I'm telling you for the last time, don't ever call me Tiny!"

"Babe?" Jason turned to her, laying on the charm. "I'm sorry. I didn't know—"

"Yes, you did," Nina said. Julia heard tears swelling in her best friend's voice. "You know how it makes me feel. I'm not helpless, Jason. Don't treat me like I am." She wiped her eyes, then said, "I think you'd better leave."

But Jason had come for Nina, and Julia knew firsthand that he wouldn't easily leave without her.

"Nina, honey, I worry about you," Jason said. He reached

for her hand and began massaging her small fingers. "We're no good without each other. It's always been you and me. Forever, remember? What do you say? Come on, let's go talk about this."

Julia's heart lodged in her throat as she saw her best friend teeter on the brink of what could possibly be the most important decision of her life. Down one path was a fictional night at the movies with her ex-husband. Down the other lay a night of burglary with her best friend. No matter which way Nina turned, danger and adventure waited.

Nina pulled her fingers from Jason's grasp, and Julia began to breathe again.

"Whatever you have to say to me, you can say here, in front of my friends, or you can say it to my lawyer." Nina wiped her eyes. "It's your choice."

"But, Tiny . . ." Jason started.

"Don't call her that!" Julia roared and stepped closer.

"Get away from me, bitch." Jason sneered, shoving Julia into the wall. She crashed and felt her elbow bang sharply, as Lance stepped between Jason and Nina, expertly sliding her out of harm's way.

He sounded calm when he said, "Looks like he's chosen the lawyer route, Nina." Lance placed one hand on Jason's shoulder, a friendly gesture with decidedly unfriendly implications. His voice was low and steady as he spoke near Jason's ear: "Nina doesn't want to talk to you. She doesn't want to see you. And even more than that, I don't want to see you. If you come near any of these women again, I'll hear about it. Do you understand me?" When Jason didn't reply, Lance shook him gently, as if trying to wake a sleeping child. "I asked if you understood."

"Yes." Jason grimaced.

"Okay. Now, remember, if you want to give me a go, all you have to do is say one word to any of these women, and we'll see who the tough guy really is."

Caroline already had the door open, so Lance gave Jason a small shove, and Jason stumbled onto the porch. He didn't have time to say anything, much less comprehend what had just happened, before Caroline closed the door and flipped the lock.

Lance turned and asked Nina, "You okay?" When she nodded, he turned his attention to Julia. "What about you?"

Julia's elbow was tender and it hurt. She looked at the closed door that Jason was locked behind and thought for one terrifying second what might have happened if Lance hadn't been there.

"Julia," Lance asked, snapping her back to the moment. "Are you okay?"

She nodded, and Lance said, "Good." Then he turned away and began climbing the stairs, wrapped in a cloak of quiet confidence. He hadn't yelled his warning, he'd whispered it, and Julia knew the sound of his voice would be reverberating in Jason's ears for years.

*So men like that really do exist. So that's what all the fuss is about.*

◆

At one fifteen they synchronized their watches. Julia didn't
know exactly why, but it still felt like the thing to do. Then Julia, Nina, and Lance checked the batteries in their flashlights
one last time and said good-bye to Caroline, who was already
holding a sleeping Nicholas.

As they prepared to go, Julia watched Lance from the corner of her eye. If things went wrong, the consequences would
be worst for him—he was a strong, able-bodied man breaking
into the home of an elderly woman. She and Nina posed a far
lesser physical threat. Plus, they could always plead insanity
and, judging from their recent and extended history, most ju-
ries would buy it.

Nina had gone downstairs first, following Caroline's instructions to test the walkie-talkie on the far side of the lawn
to best gauge its range and volume, so Julia and Lance were
alone as they left the playroom. When they reached the first-
floor landing, Julia took his arm and said, "Can I talk to you
for a second?"

He looked a little surprised by her timing, but stopped and
said, "Okay."

"What you did for Nina—it's going to change her life.
I just want to thank you and tell you that I appreciate it."

A wry smile stretched across his face as if he'd just cracked
her code. Julia had never felt so naked with her clothes on.
"What?" she muttered.

"That was hard for you, wasn't it?"

"No, of course not. I'm a gracious person."

"I know," he said. "You're a thanker."

She didn't know what he meant by that, but it didn't sound like an insult, so she let it slide. "Anyway, I want you to know that I appreciate all that you've done, and that as far as I'm concerned, we're even. You don't have to do this. It should be easy enough, and it shouldn't take three of—"

"You're right," he cut her off. "You stay here."

"Wait!" She grabbed him. "I mean *you* should stay. It's my problem. I'll fix it."

"We've already spent one night in jail together, Julia. I don't see why we should go for two."

An all-too-realistic vision flashed in Julia's mind—fifteen years on a hard bench with thumbtacks poking into her skull.

Only his grin could snap her back into the moment. He leaned close and said, "Breathe."

"Lance, what I'm trying to say is that it's okay. I can handle this one. You don't need to take the risk."

"Julia, I get the risks—believe me. If it were up to me, you wouldn't be going over there at all. So you can wait here while I go get your manuscript, or you can come with me. Personally, I'd prefer it if you and Nina would stay put."

"Out of the question."

"Then after you." He made a show of stepping back and sweeping his arms toward the patio doors.

# Chapter Twenty-one

*There's a full moon over Tulsa/I hope that it's shining on you*, David Frizzell sang inside Julia's mind as she stood on Caroline's patio and stared into the face of the largest full moon she'd ever seen. *So much for the cover of darkness.* It shone a spotlight on everything—sandboxes, Big Wheels, and the half-finished fence that marked the point of no return beyond Caroline's backyard.

Nina emerged from the shadows of the patio, and the three of them surveyed the scene like a battlefield, their eyes scanning for snipers or land mines or worse, Cassie's Bubble Fun Push Mower, which lit up and played music anytime you touched it.

Then, as if moved by the hand of God, a dense cloud swept across the night sky, blotting out the moon. The three of them bolted, like lightning, for the fence. They stood side-by-side with their backs flat against the completed section, breathing hard. Julia fought the feeling that they were practicing for a police lineup. Beside her, she heard Lance's steady breathing and felt his arm press against hers.

"Last chance to turn back," she said, more for his benefit than Nina's, but Lance was already gone, ducking quickly and silently around the end of the fence. All she and Nina could do was follow.

Darting across Myrtle's backyard, Julia's heart was pounding. *Am I this out of shape?* she wondered, feeling as though she were trying to breathe water. She'd never been so grateful to see a wall in her life as when they reached the house and dropped to their knees next to Lance, who was already crouched beneath the unlocked window. She heard the walkie-talkie crackle, and it sounded like a freight train in the silence.

"Windows are black," Caroline said. "We are a go."

*When this is over,* Julia decided, *I'm sending Caroline on a very long, very exotic vacation.*

She leaned against the cranberry-colored brick that covered every wall in the development. The window above her was double-paned and double-hung, but luckily, it didn't have a screen. Lance looked at Nina then locked eyes with Julia, an unspoken "get out of here" passing between them. But Julia nodded toward the glass, and his gaze changed to "here goes nothing." He applied gentle pressure to the window, and it eased silently up. Beside her, Julia could feel Nina gloating. Lance turned to Nina, who tucked the walkie-talkie into the zipper pocket of her black fleece pullover. He leaned over and cupped his hands, and she gave him her right foot as if they'd practiced the maneuver a hundred times before. Her hands went to Lance's shoulders. With no more breath than a whisper, he said, "One, two . . ." On three, he lifted until her head, shoulders, and waist disappeared into the darkened window, and Nina shimmied the rest of the way inside.

Julia listened for a crash. In movies, there's always some kind of shatter as the person going through the window lands on a stray pot or sleeping cat. Nothing. The silence seemed imminently worse. Julia couldn't help herself—she leaned into the window and whispered, "Nina!" but Lance clamped his hand over her mouth before she could make another sound. She tasted the rubber of his latex gloves and felt his warm breath on the back of her neck as he whispered, "Wait."

Her eyes stayed glued to the black, empty expanse of the kitchen and keeping room. *Where was Nina?* Fear boiled inside Julia. She strained to see something inside the darkened house. She was about to fight free of Lance's grip and call out for her best friend again, when Lance turned her to face the backyard, where Nina stood on the dewy grass, hands on hips, a "what are you waiting for?" expression on her pinched face.

Lance took Julia's hand and led her around the corner of the house. They'd gone patio door to patio door in less than two minutes. The *Italian Job* people didn't have anything on them.

As they stepped into the keeping room, Julia knew for certain that Myrtle wasn't playing with a full deck. The mess that filled the room went far beyond sloth. Julia looked at the mountains of junk on every free surface and became impressed that Nina had made it silently through the obstacle course that lay between the keeping room and the patio doors. Old newspapers were stacked everywhere, each pile two or three feet tall. Julia did some quick calculations and remembered that Caroline and Steve had moved in at the end of the summer, roughly eight months before. Myrtle had moved in at about the same time, and Julia guessed from looking at the piles of papers that the woman hadn't thrown a single one away during all that time. The sight of all the newspapers made Julia cringe with the thought of how difficult it might be to find the manuscript if it was anywhere other than in its box, and if the box was somewhere other than the garage.

She felt a tug on her sleeve and turned to see Lance wordlessly urging her forward. Nina was already trotting into the kitchen, dodging unopened bags of flour and cases of canned food. She moved as though the bulk groceries were laser beams, using the swift, precise motions of someone who's watched way too many episodes of *Alias*.

*Better make it an exotic vacation for two*, Julia decided, realizing that both Nina and Caroline needed to find a legal outlet for their energy.

Lance and Julia followed Nina's lead, with far less precision. When the three of them reached the door that led to the garage, Lance placed his hand on the knob, and Julia felt him silently count to three. Then he opened the door, and they all piled in, with perfect SWAT team precision. Well, almost perfect.

Lance collided with a bicycle. Nina knocked a rake, a hoe, and a snow shovel off a rack. Julia stubbed her toe and tumbled onto the hood of Myrtle's Cadillac. For a minute, they were all as quiet as church mice, looking at each other through the diluted glow of Lance's flashlight.

"Caroline," Nina whispered into the walkie-talkie. "Caroline," she said again, risking a little more volume. "Do you see lights?" she asked, then nervously added, "Over."

Julia's mind flashed back to the diagrams spread across the changing table. She recalled the layout of the first floor, remembering that the master bedroom was upstairs—*upstairs, above the garage*. Ridiculous excuses logjammed in her mind. *Oh, yes, officers, we're the community yard-sale committee . . . termite inspectors . . . sleepwalkers?*

"Caroline?" Nina asked again, this time not hiding the panic that they were all beginning to feel. A long, eerie silence followed before Caroline's static-riddled voice came through the walkie-talkie. "Sorry guys. Nick was wet."

"Caroline," Nina snapped, *"are there lights?"*

A terribly long moment passed while, presumably, Caroline checked the window. "You're clear, Alpha team, proceed as planned. Operation is a go."

"*Alpha team*"? Maybe it wasn't a vacation Caroline needed—maybe it was thera—

"Pit bull!" Nina hissed.

Julia spun around to see a big brown dog in a spiked leather collar standing at the top of the concrete stairs. The dog was looking at them as if it didn't know whether they were intruders or circus performers hired for his entertainment. Its front legs were perched on top of a giant bag of dog food. In the glare of the flashlight Julia could just make out the swinging flap of the doggie door.

"Oh, boy," Lance said. He eased toward the now-growling animal. "Hey, boy," he said. "How ya doing there, big guy? You don't need to bark. No. You don't need to bark." Then Julia saw Lance's hand move to his pocket, and moments later he was holding an uncooked hot dog. With a gentle flick, he tossed it onto the concrete landing. But the dog was unsure which piece of meat looked better, the weenie or Lance; it looked between the two of them, sniffing. Then it lowered its head and began to eat.

Julia watched in amazement, but Nina summed it up best: "Holy crap."

Lance didn't stop to marvel at his accomplishment. Instead, he turned to them and whispered, "Let's get out of here, quick. I've only got a few more with me."

"How did you know to bring hot dogs?" Nina asked.

He raised his eyebrows. "Not all crazy people lie."

"Okay," Julia said. "Let's spread out and find that manuscript. It's in a medium-sized brown box."

"You mean like those brown boxes?" Nina said and turned. The beam of her flashlight swept across the garage, illuminating a mountainous pile of boxes, each nearly identical to the one Myrtle had hauled from Caroline's curb.

"What kind of freak *is* she?" Julia asked, no longer trying to mask her voice.

"The kind who's gonna send us to prison if she finds us," Lance said softly. "Now let's look and get out of here."

With the mountain before them, it was pretty safe to assume that new arrivals were at the top. Plus, upon closer inspection, Julia noticed that not all of the boxes were plain or brown. Some had mailing labels, or black-and-white pictures of TVs and computer monitors, with instructions written in English, Spanish, and Japanese.

"It was plain?" Lance asked.

"Yes. A plain brown box. No writing of any kind. Probably two feet square."

"Like that one?" Nina asked, and sent a beam of light upward to a shelf that must have been fifteen feet above the concrete floor. The three of them stood with their heads craned back so far that they could have seen straight up to Heaven if it hadn't been for Myrtle's bedroom directly above them.

"How in the world did she get it up there?" Julia asked.

"You're sure that's the one?" Lance asked.

There wasn't a doubt in Julia's mind.

Lance steadied a ladder while Julia climbed almost to its highest rung, teetering. *Don't look down, don't look down,* she chanted to herself. She pried open the four corners of the box and, with a mini-flashlight in her mouth, saw what she hadn't seen in years. She pulled out early drafts of *Table for One*, old short stories she desperately wanted to stop and read, letters she'd received from Caroline and Nina that had inspired her to keep writing.

"We don't have time for a stroll down memory lane," Nina whispered. "Find the blasted book!"

Julia dug in again, wincing with paper cuts as her hands slid down between the pages, until panic began to set in. "It's not in here. I don't believe it. It's not . . ."

"Are you sure?" Lance asked.

"It's not in here!"

"Get down," Lance said, gesturing to the safety of the floor.

She stared down at him, so calm and safe on the ground beneath her, then she considered hurling herself off the ladder. *Better to end the humiliation here.*

"Just get down," he soothed. "We'll figure something out."

Julia began the long descent. At the base of the ladder, Nina put her arm around Julia's shoulders to comfort her as Lance asked, "What was it in?"

"That box," she cried, pointing again to the top shelf.

"I mean the manuscript, specifically. It wasn't just loose in there, was it?"

"No," Julia said, remembering. "It was in one of those accordion-type files that expands and has a flap that goes over and a piece of cord that wraps around."

"Okay," Lance said. "You and Nina are going to go home now, and I'm going to go into the house and look for that file."

"Nuh-uh," Nina said.

"Three of us will be three times faster," Julia suggested.

"Yes, and three times louder," Lance replied. "That triples our chances of getting caught, and we haven't exactly been good at this so far."

"I'm not leaving you," Julia said defiantly.

"Me either," Nina said, sounding offended that she might get cut out of her own master plan.

Lance looked at them, seemingly weighing his options. "Fine. But we're just doing the downstairs. Agreed?"

Nina and Caroline looked at each other. "Agreed," they said in unison.

Lance handed the dog another weenie, and they were heading into the kitchen when Nina stopped and said, "My flashlight! I laid it down to help hold the ladder. I'll be right back."

"No," Lance said. "You two go on. I'll get it."

He disappeared before the walkie-talkie came to life with Caroline's muffled cry: "Abort!"

Julia and Nina froze.

Again, Caroline hissed, "Abort! Abort! Abort!"

Julia looked around for Lance; Nina was running in place, rotating from the waist up like a compass spinning out of control looking for north. All Julia could think of was Lance, finding Lance, getting Lance out of there.

"Closet!" Nina grabbed Julia and squeezed in beside her

just as light came streaming through the frosted glass of the pantry door.

"Who's there?" Myrtle yelled. "You! Who are you?"

*No!* Julia thought but couldn't scream. She saw a solid, six-two form walk in front of the frosted glass.

"Oh, hoo!" Myrtle squealed like a schoolgirl. "This is so exciting! I knew my Johnny wouldn't forget my birthday," she said. "Every year he does this!" she exclaimed with glee. "Every year he gets me a stripper!"

# Chapter Twenty-two

"I've heard of cop strippers before, but you must be a new
kind," Myrtle said, pondering it. "You must be a robber
stripper!"

Lance tried to remember the cab ride. He'd heard a good
offer from a beautiful woman, but somehow that cab had
brought him to a cluttered kitchen where he was being propo-
sitioned by a geriatric klepto. *Next time,* Lance told himself,
*keep walking.*

"So, whatcha waiting on? Neither one of us is getting any
younger."

Caroline had been right about the whiskey, Lance realized.

Myrtle was sloshed. She wasn't stumbling or slurring her words like a cheap, once-in-a-blue-moon drunk. Instead, she had the body control of a full-fledged alcoholic. Lance knew both kinds of drunks better than he would have liked; that's something that comes with the territory when working behind a bar. Who can drive? Who can't? Who's faking sobriety? Myrtle was an accomplished fake, but her glazed expression and ruddy skin betrayed her. The fact that she had two different color socks peeking out from beneath her hot-pink muumuu didn't help her case, either.

Lance was formulating a plan when he heard the faint hum of walkie-talkie static and knew immediately that the situation was even worse than he'd thought—Julia and Nina were still in the house.

"My Johnny didn't pay you to stand," Myrtle bellowed, shaking her curler-covered head. Then she began chanting, "*Strip. Strip. Strip. Strip.*"

"I think maybe we should go in here," Lance said loudly, and began to steer her out of the kitchen, away from the sounds of static and spilling cereal. "I think it would be best if you sat here, with your back to the patio doors," he practically yelled. "There. That's perfect. You just sit there and keep your *eyes on me.*"

"That's our cue!" Julia said to Nina.

She eased the pantry door open just in time to hear Lance yell, "Wait! Why are you going *to the kitchen?*"

*Okay, already,* Julia thought. *We're not deaf.* She eased the door closed.

"I can't believe that old bat gets to see him naked," Nina complained as she and Julia stood, cramped and motionless. "If anyone should get to see him naked, it's us. We're the ones who—"

"Got him into this mess," Julia said, shutting Nina up.

They heard heavy footsteps outside, then the clank of ice in a glass and a bottle opening. Julia smelled liquor and hoped that Myrtle would continue in her alcoholic stupor and wake tomorrow morning thinking the whole thing had been a dream. She also hoped the old bat wouldn't look in the pantry. She didn't want to think about what else Myrtle might be looking at by the end of the night.

"Don't you boys usually bring music?" Myrtle yelled.

"Oh, but I'm a robber stripper," Lance said. "I'm supposed to *steal* music from you."

Myrtle seemed pleased by the sound of that. "Sure," she said. "Just let me put on an album."

Julia heard the shuffling of feet going to the far end of the kitchen, and then nothing. A long moment passed before the door flew open.

"Ah!" she and Nina gasped. Julia held up a hand to shield herself against the glare of Lance's flashlight.

"Get out!" Lance hissed, dragging Julia by the arm toward the door. "Now! Go! Get!" And with one solid push, they were locked on the other side of Crazy Myrtle's patio doors. Julia turned and bolted away from the glass, but Nina stayed behind. "Do you think she'd notice if we stood here and watched?" she asked.

♠

"Why isn't he back yet?" Julia asked while pacing a hole in the playroom carpet.

"Maybe he takes it off real slow," Nina said from her post by the telescope.

"Nina!" Julia cried, then realized her best friend had a point. *Let's see . . . if it takes a minute per shoe, two minutes for a shirt? Pants? How long for the pants?* She gave herself a mental slap.

"I can't see any of the good stuff through this thing," Nina said, but she still didn't offer to let anyone else take a turn at the telescope. Caroline had nearly passed out when Myrtle's lights came on, and when Julia and Nina came back to the house, she was more than happy to hand over central control duties to Nina while she rested on the couch and let her heart slow down to a normal pace.

Julia, however, was getting more nervous by the second. "I've got this terrible feeling in my gut."

Nina cut her eyes toward Julia and said, "You've got a weird feeling all right, but I'm betting it's not in your gut. I'm betting you're nice and tingly all over."

"This is serious, Nina! Like jail time serious. What if Myrtle figures out what's really going on? What if the dog is allergic to hot dogs?"

"What dog?" a bewildered Caroline wanted to know.

Julia plowed by her sister's question. "What if she thinks he's supposed to do more than dance?"

"Well, we're gonna find out." Nina turned from the telescope. "He's leaving."

♣

Three different looks on three different faces told Lance all he needed to know as soon as he walked into Caroline's huge house. Nina was standing at attention, a human paper towel, ready to absorb all the juicy details. Caroline was resting in an overstuffed chair, her feet propped on an ottoman and her eyelids fluttering as exhaustion slowly won the battle with intrigue. But Julia's face was priceless.

"What took you so long?" she said before he'd even closed the patio door. "Don't tell me you were stripping all that time, because you're not wearing that many clothes!"

As much as Lance was enjoying the look on her face, he thought it was time to ease her mind a little. "I looked for the manuscript," he said. "I couldn't find it. I'm sorry."

"What?" she asked, confused.

"The manuscript," he reminded her. "I couldn't find it."

"So you're okay?" she demanded.

"Yes," he told her, slightly taken aback.

"You scared me half to death," she said, and Lance thought he sensed something like affection in her tone. She tried to smack his shoulder as a punishment, but he caught her wrists in his hands and pulled her toward him.

"Myrtle," he spoke softly, calmly, "is a sentimental drunk."

"She cried afterwards, didn't she?" Nina jumped in.

But Lance's gaze never left Julia. "You know that stuff in her house, all those mountains of junk we had to dodge all night?" he asked.

"Yes," Julia said.

"Well, there's a story behind it. Every piece of it. There are stories about the stories. I got to hear them all."

"But was this naked listening? Semi-naked? Can you give us a visual?" Nina asked.

"Nina," Lance said, turning to face her, "a gentleman never tells."

♥

After dozing most of the night on the sofa in the playroom, Julia woke once again to the sight of Nina and Caroline staring out a window.

"Aunt Julia!" Cassie cried as she plowed through the playroom and jumped into Julia's arms. The little girl was still in her pajamas, her wild hair frizzing all around and tickling Julia's nose as she gave her a huge hug. "Come on," Cassie said, sliding down Julia's hip to the floor. "Let's go play in my room."

"No, honey," Caroline said. "Aunt Julia can't play right now."

"Caroline, I'll . . ." Julia started, but stopped cold when she read her sister's expression. Then she turned her attention to her niece. "You go on, sweetie. I'll be in after I talk to your momma."

Cassie darted down the hall, and Julia crept toward the window.

"He's back," Caroline whispered, urgency rising in her voice. "He's in the house . . . Richard Stone!"

Julia rushed to the window just in time to see Lance's agent appear on Myrtle's porch and shake the woman's hand. Then he turned and began walking down the sidewalk toward a car, an accordion-style folder tucked under one arm.

Without thinking, Julia flew down the stairs in bare feet and her burglary outfit from the night before. Sleep and fatigue clung to her, and a disgusting taste filled her mouth, but she knew that she had to stop that man before he drove away. She was at the base of the stairs and through the entryway in a matter of seconds. She saw him step toward his car that was parked across the street, so she hurled herself off the porch. In the middle of the street, Richard Stone stopped and stared at her, dumbfounded.

"*Stone!*" she yelled.

She stumbled into the street and clung to the front bumper of his car. But the agent merely eased closer to the car door and broke into a laugh. "Well, if it isn't the blushing bride," he said. "Now, you need to be careful. All this physical exertion might not be good for someone in your delicate condition." He opened the car door and stood so that he was shielded by the big piece of metal and glass.

"I believe you have something *that belongs to me*," Julia said.

"This?" he asked, chuckling. He held up the folder that contained the manuscript, then tossed it casually onto the passenger seat of the car. "My friend Myrtle found that and thought I might like to read it. I'm looking forward to it. I just can't help but wonder why a big, bestselling author like you would want to publish under any other name. But, babe, I'm really looking forward to finding out."

Julia clawed her way onto the hood of the car. "*You're not leaving here, Stone!*" she yelled. "*You're not getting away with . . .*"

The car must have been newly waxed, because Julia, in her black cotton burglary gear, was sliding farther and farther down the hood. She tried to crawl up, but every time she moved forward six inches, she'd slide back a foot. Julia had to press her cheek to the warm hood of the vehicle and brace her feet against the hood ornament to maintain any kind of traction at all.

"You're not getting away. . . ."

She heard the engine start and felt the hood begin to vibrate as she lost her grip and slid to the street, and a split second later, both Richard Stone and Veronica White were gone.

# Chapter Twenty-three

"Julia, honey, I've got biscuits and gravy. You love biscuits and gravy," Caroline was saying as Lance followed a wonderful aroma into the kitchen.

"Here, honey, have some juice. You like juice," Caroline reminded her sister.

"Jules," Nina chimed, "no one could have stopped him."

"Stop who? Not . . ." Lance asked, but one look at the three faces around the island told him that his agent had indeed come calling. He tried to focus on the humor of the situation, because if he thought about anything else, he was afraid he'd be tempted to lose himself in the pan of homemade biscuits that Nina was pulling out of the oven. "Why didn't someone get me?"

"It happened too fast for that," Nina said. "It just happened too fast." She went to the refrigerator, but Lance didn't know what could possibly be left in there—the kitchen counter was already overflowing.

"And Myrtle gave him the manuscript?" he asked.

"Yes. He's got it," Caroline said. She turned to her sister. "That which does not kill us makes us stronger. Right?"

Julia didn't respond. She just looked blankly ahead.

Lance studied her. It wasn't just her puffy eyes that weighed on him—it was the overall feel of her that made him worry. Gone was the steadfast woman who'd seemed at ease with the world while sitting alone at Stella's; missing was the gracious celebrity who'd signed autographs, the caring aunt who'd bought half the inventory of FAO Schwarz. The protective layer that had kept Julia calm and serene had been stripped away, and what was left was something far too fragile to exist in the world.

For Julia, a career wasn't a livelihood; it was an identity. Lance looked at her and realized that if Julia James and Veronica White ever tried to exist on the same plane, one of them would have to die, and he couldn't let that happen.

"Nina, can I borrow your car?" he asked.

Nina reemerged from the freezer, looking as though she'd developed a mild case of frostbite. "Why?"

"I just . . ." he started. "There's just something I need to do."

◆

Evidently, Tammy with the great eyes and love for Thai food hadn't skipped the country entirely, because she was the person who answered the phone when Lance called the offices of Poindexter-Stone in New York. It had taken a little persuading, but eventually she told him what he needed to know, and that was how he found himself poised outside room number two-fifteen at a motel outside of Tulsa. He raised his hand to knock, but his fist hung involuntarily in midair. *Maybe I could sweet-talk a maid into letting me into the room? I might get lucky and find the manuscript just lying there, unattended and ready to be taken.* But then Lance shook his head. Nina was starting to rub off on him. This was a serious problem. It required a serious solution.

After Lance had talked to Tammy, he'd called his mother and laid out all the details of the bargain he was prepared to make with Richard Stone. She had actually cried, not because she was upset but because she was very proud. And very theatrical. His mother had proclaimed that he was prepared to fall on his sword to save the woman he cared about, but standing on the motel balcony, Lance didn't feel noble. Instead, he felt like a failure, like someone who doesn't keep his promises, even the ones he has made to himself.

*I did this,* Lance admitted. *I conned my way into Stella's,* he remembered, taking responsibility for the first in a series of lies that had changed Julia's life and exposed her secret, and now he was willing to break one promise to keep another—the promise that he'd never take advantage of her again. He raised his hand to the door. He knocked.

"I've been doing some very interesting reading," Richard Stone said after he'd opened the door and gotten over his surprise at seeing Lance. "What I can't figure out is whether the two of you have known each other for years, and she wrote this about you then, or if you're just a dream come true." He snickered.

The room fit the man, dated and dingy. Lance stepped inside onto the shag carpet as Richard went on.

"So, what is it? Long-lost love? College fling?"

"You know that's not the way it is," Lance shot back.

And with that, Richard Stone's snicker evolved into a full laugh. "Oh, you are so serious. Only dramas for you. No comedies." Richard slipped his glasses on and looked back down at the manuscript pages. Then, glancing up, he asked Lance, "Do you think she still has the film rights to this, because with you starring—"

"I want you to give that to me," Lance said and held out his hand.

Richard laughed. "That's a good one." His gaze dropped again, and he began flipping through the dog-eared pages. "That woman of yours is very ingenious. In fact, I've got some buddies who'd probably love . . ."

"I came for the manuscript," Lance said. He heard his own voice ripple with tension. "I'm not leaving without it."

"Now, that sounds like love talking to me," Richard said,

eyebrows raised. "Did you know there is a whole other level of parts I can get for you if you really love her—some honey stuff?"

"I came for the manuscript," Lance said again, growing stronger in his resolve.

"You want this, do you?" the little man asked, holding the pages away from Lance's reach. "Well, I don't think I'm going to give it to you." He went to the dresser, picked up a handful of scripts, and tossed them onto the bed in front of Lance, where they landed, splayed like a deck of cards. "Your stock has already started to fall. So, no, I don't think I'll be giving you this manuscript today. I think the world might need to hear about the *true* adventures of Philippe and Isabella. Or," Richard said, drawing one hand to his lips, "should I say Lance and Julia?" He turned back to the manuscript. "Page one-fifty-seven alone should—"

"You don't need the manuscript," Lance said.

"Oh, yes I do," Richard cried.

"No, you don't."

"Why?" Richard asked, tempting Lance to trump his hand.

Lance straightened. His voice was clear and steady as he said, "Because I'm willing to make a trade."

Then he sat down on the bed and gathered the scripts and told Richard Stone what he had spent five years hoping no one would ever find out.

# Chapter Twenty-four

> **WAY #97: Choose very carefully the bridges you burn.**
> One of the challenges of being single is making major deci-
> sions without a sounding board. No matter how certain you
> are that you're doing the right thing, realize that sometimes
> you're going to need to turn around.
>
> —from *101 Ways to Cheat at Solitaire*

"Good-bye chapter seven!" Julia cried as she tossed the pages into the fireplace and watched the flames lick at their edges, reducing *Tomorrow's Temptation* to dust. "Tell me how you got it again," she asked, pulling her legs beneath her, curling up like a child in front of the fire.

"I bribed a maid into letting me into his hotel room," Lance answered. "He was in the shower, so I grabbed the manuscript and got out."

"But not before you . . ." she prompted.

"Took all his clothes," Lance obliged, biting back a smile. "And . . ."

"All the towels."

"And then you . . ."

"Threw them in the swimming pool."

Julia threw both arms skyward, signaling *touchdown* with her hands, then fed another handful of pages to the flames. "The swimming pool part is my favorite. Nina's very proud."

"It felt very *Nina* when I was doing it. You know who else would have approved? The Georgias."

Julia agreed. "The Georgias would have loved every second."

"And Ro-Ro," Lance offered.

But Julia was shaking her head. "Ro-Ro would have taken the sheets, too."

Lance laughed. "I could learn a lot from Ro-Ro."

The light from the fire mixed with the sound of his laughter and seemed to wash over her old house. She held the next set of pages out to Lance. "Chapter eight?" she offered, but he shook his head.

"Count Sebastian rides into town in chapter eight. Without him, Isabella wouldn't have realized her true love for Philippe. Now, do you really want to do that to Count Sebastian?"

"You bet your life I do. He was a little vagrant. Burn, baby, burn!" she said, tossing the pages into the fire and watching the flames dance with fresh fuel. Julia rose to her knees and yelled at the top of her lungs, knowing there wasn't a soul for five miles in any direction to hear her, "Veronica White is retired! Veronica White is dead!"

She turned to him, prepared to laugh, but he was staring. Julia felt burned herself beneath his gaze, and her cheeks flushed. She felt bare, without any of the defenses she had spent years mastering.

"You're not really burning her, you know," Lance said. "You're still her."

"But no one can prove it," she said, praying it was true.

He moved closer and said, "I can."

She looked at him, and things grew very quiet, the only sound the sparking of the fire. He grasped the loose pages of the manuscript. "A real woman wrote this," he said. "A *person*, not a made-up name and a black-and-white picture. It has your fingerprints all over it, Julia. You said that yourself. Don't pretend that Veronica's dead." He moved closer.

"Lance," she started, but the feel of his hands around her waist made her stop.

"Tell me I can kiss you," he said, moving his hands to the sides of her face. "Tell me I can do this. Tell me you can feel it."

But Julia's mind was completely blank, her body numb, until Lance tilted his head and moved closer and everything came back in a flood of emotion and thought. Her mind went from empty to overflowing. She got to her feet, almost stumbling under the weight of her own body. She knew she had to get away. She had to run. She had to flee this man before she dissolved completely and forgot her own name.

He grabbed her wrist. "Stop, Julia," he said. "Just stop."

*Stop what? Stop running? Stop being myself?*

"Talk to me," Lance pleaded. "Tell me what happened to you. Tell me what I have to do to fix it!"

*Fix what?* Julia wanted to proclaim. *I'm not broken!* But as she looked down at Lance, and at the last shreds of Veronica White that lay scattered around him like last fall's leaves, words failed her. She knew how quickly everything you know can turn to ash. She couldn't meet his gaze. "Goodnight," she said. She pulled away and started for the stairs. "And thank you. For everything."

♠

The next morning, Julia peeked down the stairs. She snuck into the kitchen, her sights set on a box of granola bars and a carton of orange juice, wondering how long she could survive on that alone, thinking she might grab some crackers while she was at it.

She'd made it to the pantry door when a voice cut through the early-morning stillness of the kitchen. "I called New York."

Julia stopped dead in her tracks, frozen mid-creep, terrified of turning around. *How am I supposed to look at him?*

"Things are starting to cool down there." Lance said simply. "I think I can leave."

"Oh," Julia said, turning, despite her best efforts otherwise.

"The heat's off," he said as if the night before hadn't happened at all. "You're probably ready to have me out of your hair anyway." He looked at her from the corner of his eye as he rinsed a cereal bowl and slid it into the dishwasher.

"You're leaving?" she asked.

"Well," Lance said coolly, "there's not much reason to stay. We got the manuscript back. The press has cooled off. I don't want to outstay my welcome."

"Fine," Julia snapped without meaning to.

"Hey." He stepped forward. "What's wrong with you?"

"What's wrong with me? What's wrong with me?" she asked, stalling while she thought, *What* is *wrong with me?* "I'll tell you what's wrong with me. . . ."

The phone began to ring. She picked up and said hello.

"Julia, it's your mother. I've got bad news."

# Chapter Twenty-five

When Julia walked into the Fitzgerald Wing of Mercy General Hospital, she noticed that someone had been very skilled at spending Ro-Ro's money. Even Nina would have approved of the beautiful-yet-comfortable chairs. But no matter how lavish its furnishings, the place still smelled like death. She wondered if Lance could smell it, too.

When they got into an elevator and waited for the doors to close, Lance pushed the button for the eighth floor, then eased his arm around Julia's shoulders. The weight of his arm felt good, so she sank into him, grateful for someone to lean on.

"I think it's going to take a lot more than a fall to hurt Ro-Ro," Lance said, as if he knew she needed to hear it. But Julia couldn't forget the tone of her mother's voice on the phone. She'd had sixty miles to process, sixty miles to think, but standing in that elevator with Lance's arm around her shoulders, Julia still struggled with the realization that the impossible had happened—that Ro-Ro, after all, was human.

"Fitzgerald was husband number . . ." Lance prompted.

"Four," Julia answered. "The doctor-slash-medical-researcher."

Lance nodded as if it was something he had known but forgotten. "So, what does a twenty-million-dollar donation buy you in health care today, besides the chance to wield those really big scissors at the ribbon-cutting ceremony?" he asked, and Julia had to smile.

The doors opened and she said, "I guess we'll find out."

They started down the hall but couldn't see any uniformed footmen standing outside room 862 to take coats and introduce guests. There wasn't a gold placard on the wall, proclaiming that to be the Fitzgerald Suite. In fact, when Julia peeked inside, all she saw was an ordinary hospital room, complete with bad linens, uncomfortable chairs, and a plastic water pitcher on the bedside table. When they entered the room, it was so dim that Julia could barely see the frail woman beneath the sheets, covered with IV tubes and hospital bracelets and, of course, the four largest diamonds Julia had ever seen.

"Hi, Aunt Rosemary," she whispered, half out of respect and somber purpose, half out of nerves. "How are you feeling?"

"How do you think I'm feeling?" the old woman snapped, and with that, Julia's fears subsided. *Ro-Ro feels like bitching— all is right with the world!* "They brought me here in that horrible contraption with all those lights and sirens. They woke up the neighbors. The whole building saw me carried out like an invalid! I'll never be able to show my face there again."

*Miss Georgia will be glad to hear it,* Julia thought.

She inched closer to the bed and looked at the massive cast that surrounded Ro-Ro's left leg. She wanted to ask her if it hurt, or take the felt-tip pen she kept in her bag for autographing books and sign Ro-Ro's pristine bandages. But before she could do any such thing, Ro-Ro looked behind Julia and spoke to Lance. "You're still here I see."

Lance inched forward and said, "Yes, ma'am. I'm here for a little while longer."

"Nonsense," Ro-Ro dismissed him.

Julia looked between Lance and Ro-Ro and wondered why her aunt would say such a thing. Then Julia's mother came floating into the room and whispered, "They have her on d-r-u-g-s."

"I broke my leg, not my ears, Madelyn," Ro-Ro lorded over them from the bed.

Madelyn ignored her like a pro. She hugged Lance and crooned, "Oh, I'm so glad you're here." Then she swept toward her aunt and eldest daughter. "Julia, dear, thank you so much for coming."

Julia's blood went cold—Madelyn was using her "death voice"—the one she used while thanking someone for a Bundt cake and telling them when the funeral would be. Julia looked at Ro-Ro, so tiny on the bed, so frail, and she pulled her mother out into the hallway. "What's really wrong with her?" she asked once they'd closed the door behind them.

"She broke her leg while climbing out of the bathtub. I told you that on the phone."

"No, Mother, I want the whole story."

Madelyn looked down at her hands as if trying to find the balance between honesty and gossip. "She's an old woman, Julia. We're not even sure how old. She tells everyone she's eighty-six, but you can only stay eight-six for so long. I know for a fact she's over ninety."

Julia stole a glance back at Ro-Ro through the slim window in the door.

"Legs don't mend too well when you're over ninety," Madelyn went on. "Plus, she was in the bathroom when the maid found her." Madelyn grew nervous. She looked around to make sure no one could hear. "She was *naked*," Madelyn whispered, emphasizing the scandalous word at the sentence's end. "I'm surprised she hasn't had those poor paramedics' eyes gouged out yet. That's where your father is right now, meeting with the hospital heads, trying to save those poor boys' jobs."

Julia couldn't help herself. She laughed out loud.

"Julia!" her mother cried in disgrace. "Of course they covered her up before they brought her outside. But with her leg being in such bad shape, they weren't able to, you know, put on any *underwear*," she whispered.

"Ro-Ro's going commando?"

Madelyn waved at her eldest daughter, dismissing her completely as she returned to Rosemary's room, closing the door on Julia and her laughter.

"I guess you heard about the commando thing?" a voice came from behind, and Julia turned to see her sister. Julia used the back of her hands to wipe her eyes as she remembered that she was in a hospital.

"I'm a terrible person," Julia admitted.

"I laughed, too," Caroline soothed. "It just didn't hit me until I was on the elevator."

"What are you doing with that?" Julia asked, pointing to the laptop computer that Caroline was carrying.

Caroline sighed. "Now that Ro-Ro has come face-to-face with her own mortality, it's more urgent than ever that we—"

"Finish the memoirs?" Julia guessed.

Caroline nodded. "Chapter fifteen, the Cairo years. At least it can't go on much longer."

"Oh, I don't know about that. There's a lot to cover yet. Mom swears she's over ninety."

"I thought she was eighty-six," Caroline protested.

"Yeah, and she has been for a while now."

Lance came out of Ro-Ro's room and quickly shut the door behind him. He joined Julia and Caroline, and Julia thought she had seen mangled lion tamers on the Discovery Channel who looked better.

"I don't care how many drugs she's on," he said. "Someone needs to up the dosage."

"If it makes you feel any better, she's not wearing panties," Caroline told him.

A look of revulsion crossed his face. "I can *honestly* say that doesn't help."

"Caroline? Caroline?" Madelyn came running out of the room, then stopped short. "There you are! She's just remembered a joke she heard a sheikh tell at an embassy party. Bring the computer quick before she forgets the punchline."

With a roll of her eyes, Caroline followed Madelyn and disappeared into Ro-Ro's room.

Coming to visit an old friend in the hospital was a major social undertaking. After all, the Georgias were all wearing hats and carrying coordinating purses when they got off the elevator. Georgia A. was wearing a royal blue suit with a high-collared white blouse—not black, the color of mourning, but a somber, respectful choice just the same. Miss Georgia had gambled with her ensemble, daring to wear pants. Georgia B. was gunmetal gray from head to toe and looked like a cement truck.

Seeing Lance and Julia, they bolted forward. "Darling, how is she?" Georgia B. wanted to know.

Before Julia could answer, Georgia A. cut in, "I was there

when the ambulance came. And when I saw them wheel her out, oh, it just broke my heart. Broke my heart in two."

"I'm sure it was very upsetting," Julia said.

"Oh, in-deed," Georgia A. said, drawing the word out.

"She's going to fire that maid, you know," Miss Georgia chimed. "I know I would. She didn't even dry Rosemary's hair before they loaded her in the ambulance—very uncouth."

*Someone should tell her about the panties,* Lance thought.

"Well, everyone's talking about it," Georgia A. said. "The news should really run something—after all Rosemary's done."

"Maybe I should call Channel Eight?" Miss Georgia offered.

"Of course, the club should be notified," Georgia A. said. "Let's make a list, and—"

"Ladies," Julia cut them off. "She's fine. You can go see her if you'd like."

"Thank you, dear," Georgia B. said, laying a soft hand on Julia's arm. "It's nice she has *family*."

Georgia A. and Miss Georgia nodded their agreement, then they moved slowly down the hall and disappeared.

Lance settled himself in one of the chairs with a copy of *Sports Illustrated* that was six months out-of-date.

"Are you good here?" Julia asked him. "Because I should probably . . ."

He studied her, waiting for her to finish, and when she didn't, he just shooed her away with the magazine. "Go. Have fun," he mocked.

Julia rolled her eyes at him and headed toward Ro-Ro's room.

A doctor was in there now. Julia pushed the door against his long, white coat, prompting him to step forward and allow her to slide inside. Between Ro-Ro, the three Georgias, Caroline and her computer, Madelyn, and the doctor, the room was more than a little crowded.

"Julia, dear," Madelyn rushed to make introductions. "This is Dr. Tompkins. He's the Chief of Staff. He's just been in to check Rosemary's vital signs."

*The Chief of Staff*, Julia thought. *So there's at least one benefit to having your name on the side of the building.*

"Very nice to meet you," Julia said, offering the doctor her hand.

"As I was telling your mother, young lady—"

"Hump!" Ro-Ro decreed from the bed. "Walter, she is no spring chicken."

An embarrassed look flashed across Dr. Tompkins's face. Julia hurried to wave his worries away and then prompted, "You were saying, Doctor . . ."

"Yes. It seems your aunt is a very lucky lady."

Another grunt from Ro-Ro. "Luck, you say, Walter? Luck, has . . ." Ro-Ro's voice trailed off, then she snapped, "Evelyn, what *are* you doing?"

Every eye turned to Miss Georgia.

She was leaning over Ro-Ro, a curling iron in her hands.

"Well." Miss Georgia sounded guilty, as if she'd just been caught pinching a little of Ro-Ro's morphine for herself. "Rosemary, if I could just give you a little shape on the top, I know you'd feel much better." She looked to Georgia A. and Georgia B. for support, and they nodded in agreement.

As if on cue, Dr. Tompkins added, "The office of community relations *did* ask if you might consent to a photo, Mrs. Willis." *Photo!* Ro-Ro came to full attention. "After all, it isn't every day we get to treat our favorite patron," he finished with a fund-raiser's grin.

Ro-Ro surveyed the room. Julia thought she could see joy behind the old woman's scowl as she did the mental calculations, knowing she might get drugs, flowers, and press coverage all in the same day. "I suppose," Ro-Ro said slowly, "that if it will benefit the hospital, I might allow a few *tasteful* photos."

With that, Julia heard a familiar "thunk" as Miss Georgia's bag overturned, and Ro-Ro was lost in a whirlwind of Aqua Net and false eyelashes.

Every few minutes, Ro-Ro would mutter, "Evelyn, this is preposterous." But she still managed to pout, suck in her cheeks, and rub her lips together whenever Miss Georgia told her to.

♥

Waiting for the elevator in the glass atrium that led to the rooftop garden, Lance readjusted his grip on the handles of Ro-Ro's wheelchair. Since she'd already succeeded in making two nurses and a photographer cry, none of the orderlies would push her. She hummed and grinned to herself in the sunshine. By Ro-Ro's standards, it was shaping up to be a pretty good day.

Julia, Madelyn, and the rest of Ro-Ro's posse were still examining the flowers on the roof—an amazing sight, Lance had to admit, and one he hated to leave in order to return the old woman to her room. But she'd insisted, and when Ro-Ro insists . . .

"Young man, when you go back to New York—which you will—you must visit Marjorie VanGundy. She was an acting coach, one of the greats. Mention my name and she'll see to you."

The doors slid open, and Lance eased her into the elevator, but all he could think was, *What does she mean by* "which you will"?

He pushed the button, and they began their descent.

"Come stand where I can see you," she demanded. He complied. "You're too tall. Lean down." He squatted. "There. That's better," she said, but Lance didn't agree, since he was starting to lose feeling in his calves.

"Do you know why I married my four husbands?" she asked.

A proper guess would have been, "Because you loved them," but Lance felt that was too easy, so instead he shook his head and said, "No."

"When I was young, you had to be married to have freedom. It may sound silly to you, but it's true. My husbands and I traveled the world; we met interesting people, we had fascinating lives. A single woman could not have done that in my time. But"—Ro-Ro cocked her head—"*times have changed.*

An independent woman today, a woman like my niece, for example, would have *other options*. Do you understand what I'm saying?"

"Yes, ma'am," he said, meaning it.

"I know my niece well," Ro-Ro said. "We're very much alike. She has a good life, an independent life. I don't imagine that she has any reason to change it."

There was a ding, and Lance felt the doors slide open. He stood and began to push the chair into the corridor. "Yes," Ro-Ro carried on, but her tone was decidedly different. "Marjorie VanGundy might do wonderful things for you. But only if you mention my name."

◆

Julia found her mother flipping through a magazine in the waiting area down the hall from Ro-Ro's door. She sat down beside her, handed her a cup of coffee, and asked, "Is Daddy back yet?"

Madelyn closed the magazine. "He left. Didn't Lance tell you?"

"No."

"Oh, honey, they left."

"They?"

"Your father and Lance. Didn't Lance tell you he was leaving?"

♠

Julia saw the packed bag sitting by the fireplace. And there was Lance, sitting beside it.

"The cab's gonna be here soon," he said, standing up.

Julia allowed the door to slam closed behind her. She dropped her keys on a table and acted cool as she slid out of her coat and asked, "A cab? All the way out here?"

"It's really a shuttle, I guess."

"Oh. And your flight?"

"There's a six o'clock to Dallas. I can connect and be in New York by midnight." Lance took a step toward her.

"Were you going to say good-bye?"

"I was going to call you from the airport."

"Glad I made it back in time then," she said with a touch of sarcasm. She held out a hand. "It was nice knowing you. Good luck."

"Hey," Lance said, gripping her outstretched hand, pulling her closer to him. "You want me to leave. Remember? You want me out of your house and out of your life and . . ."

She wrenched her hand from his grasp. "So, what do you have lined up? Is it a play?" she asked with feigned casualness. "A movie?"

She saw him flinch, and she knew she'd hit a vein of truth.

"You can tell me," she said, wanting to ignore the alarm bells sounding in her mind. Then she looked at his bag on the floor and saw the corner of a script peeking out from the side pocket. She pointed at the pages. "Where did you get that?" she asked. *Tell me I'm wrong, Lance,* she thought. *Tell me I'm wrong.*

"Julia, it's not . . ."

"Don't tell me what it *isn't*. Tell me what it *is*," she said, but then her eyes fell to the ashes in the fireplace, to what was left of her great secret, and she realized where the script had come from. "*He* gave that to you. Didn't he?"

Guilt spread across Lance's face.

"You didn't break in and throw his clothes in the pool. You lied to me." She sank into the truth, then whispered, "You lied."

"Julia," he said, "I did what I had to do."

Then another image came to mind. "You knew last night you were going back, and still you tried . . ." Julia couldn't finish. She played through the scene again and again, wondering how she'd known that he would betray her, wishing that she hadn't been right. "Like I said, thanks for your help. Good luck." She bolted for the stairs, but Lance was instantly beside her, looking into her eyes.

"Just say you don't want me to go. All right? Just say it. Don't pick this fight, please."

"I'm not fighting. You're the one who wants to leave. I'm not standing in your way."

"Then stand in my way," he said. "If that's what you want, then stand in my way."

"What I want is my life back!" Julia cried. "I want my reputation. I want my career. I—"

"You are like a little kid!" he barked. "Spoiled. Used to having your own way—"

"Did I just hear you correctly?" she asked, her voice seeping with indignation. "Did you just infer that I am not a grown-up?"

"Yeah." He nodded his head, defiantly. "I did."

"I've been on my own for fifteen years! I've built a dynasty! I've been on *Oprah*!"

Lance pointed to her grandmother's painting that still leaned against the wall. "Where are you going to hang your picture, Julia? You've leaned it up against every wall in this house. Pick one. I'll drive the nail."

"What does that have to do with anything?"

"Thirteen cabinet knobs, Julia. Thirteen. You can't even commit to a two-dollar knob." He shook his head as the headlights of the shuttle washed across the widows facing the porch. "How did I ever expect you to commit to me?"

He grabbed his bag and walked toward the door. "Keep on playing solitaire," he told her. "Keep on staying up nights and wondering why you're too tired to get out of bed in the morning. Keep on laying out those cards, and then ask yourself when you're Ro-Ro's age if it would have been so awful to *put that painting someplace*."

The car outside honked, and Lance glanced involuntarily toward it before turning back to her. "I don't have a lot of pride, Julia, but I can't hang around here waiting just because you're not used to other people's noise."

He opened the door, then stepped onto the wide-planked porch with its peeling paint and sagging center and started for the rickety stairs. When he reached the bottom step, he turned to her. "Good-bye, Julia," he said. "And good luck. I really mean it."

Julia watched him walk away.

She stood in the cold wind until the taillights of the shuttle disappeared. Then she went inside again, locked the door, sat in front of the fireplace, and shuffled.

# Chapter Twenty-six

"If this is supposed to be a welcome-home banner made by Cassie, then why isn't Cassie making it?" Julia asked as she peeled layers of glittery glue from the ends of her fingers.

"Because it has to look nice, but like it was made by an actual five-year-old—that's why you're doing it and not Nina," Caroline said.

Julia studied the crude puffy letters and runny strips of glue and realized that if she were a five-year-old, she would never see the first grade based on her creation. She craned her head,

hoping the banner might improve with distance, but no. WEL-
COME HOME AUNT ROSEMARY was still crooked on the long
strip of yellow paper, the a-r-y of Rosemary still squished together and disproportionately small in relation to the w-e-l of
welcome. She looked across Caroline's massive dining-room
table, at the glitter and errant marker doodles covering the
newspaper they'd laid out to protect the wood, and felt certain
that Cassie herself would have been neater.

She started to pick up pieces of the newspaper and slide the
glitter into nice, uniform piles. Caroline stared at her blankly
as she worked.

"Hey, Caroline, it's okay to breathe. Ro-Ro's hired nurses,
and she's going to her own apartment when she leaves the rehab center, remember? We talked her out of coming here or to
Mom and Dad's. You don't have to take care of Ro-Ro!" But
that newsflash didn't make Caroline smile. Instead, she was
looking around her own formal dining room as if she were a
buyer at an open house.

"We *never* use this room," she said finally. "Did you know
that? We've eaten in here maybe twice in eight months.
Twice." Caroline reached under the table and came back up
with an extendible duster, which she used to reach the corners
of the twelve-foot ceiling. "Doesn't stop it from getting dirty,
though, does it?"

"Caroline," Julia started, but her sister cut her off.

"Did you know we have five bathrooms? Five?" Caroline
faced Julia. "Four people, one of whom is in diapers, live in a

house with five bathrooms." Caroline turned and began parading through her home. "Have you seen our formal living room?" she asked, arms outstretched as she walked and Julia followed. "It's very nice. It's the room we walk through on our way to the family room, which is the room we walk through to get to the kitchen, which is the room the family actually lives in."

"Caroline"—Julia grew firm—"sit down." She wrestled her sister onto one of the barstools at the granite-covered kitchen island. "Tell me what's going on."

"Oh, I hate to say it," Caroline whimpered, burying her head in her hands, "but I think Ro-Ro's right. This house is too big for us. All Steve does is work because he's worried about the mortgage. All I do is clean. We don't even see each other most days. The only way I know he's living here is because I'm still doing his laundry." Caroline was crying, but she kept talking in sharp little gasps of breath. "And we can't sell because no one wants to live in an unfinished development." She paused. *"Next to Myrtle!"*

"You'll pay down the mortgage," Julia comforted her. "And it'll get better. I can help."

Caroline looked at her, shocked. "You mean give us money?"

"We could call it a loan if that makes any difference."

"No." Caroline shook her head vigorously.

"Why not?" Julia asked. "I've got more than I'll ever need."

"Julia, we're not taking your money. Steve and I made a grown-up decision when we bought this place, and we're going to deal with it like grown-ups."

*Grown-ups.* Julia remembered the last time she'd heard that term. "It's Nick and Cassie's inheritance," Julia said bluntly. "You saw Mom. You saw the way she worried these last few weeks, spending every day at the hospital or at the rehab center because she's Ro-Ro's only family. Well, that's me, Caroline. Someday, Nick and Cassie are going to have to take care of me because I'm not going to have any kids of my own to do it. So let me help you out now."

"Julia," Caroline cried in disbelief. "You don't honestly believe that!"

"Of course I do. You know that."

"You're *nothing* like Ro-Ro," Caroline exclaimed, but Julia wasn't so sure. They were both stubborn and full of themselves, set in their ways, and growing older. She thought about Lance, the way he'd always said that Ro-Ro reminded him of someone he knew, and only then did she realize that he was talking about her.

"Caroline," Julia said slowly, "let's face it. Ro-Ro is me with better jewelry." She'd said it to be funny, but the truth hit Julia hard. When Caroline didn't laugh, Julia focused on the problem at hand. "How much would bring your payment down to a manageable level?"

Caroline didn't offer her a figure. Instead, she asked, "Have you heard from Lance?"

"Lance and I aren't pen pals, Caroline. We've gone back to our own lives like we were supposed to. Besides," Julia added, "I'm leaving for Europe in three weeks. You know how hectic book tours are, and . . ." She broke off.

"Oh, Julia."

"Caroline, it's okay. I'm going to be so busy, you wouldn't believe it. I've got to do press, and Abby wants to put out a new book really quickly, so I've got to do that. I've got to work. This is what I do, remember?"

"Yes," Caroline admitted. "It's what you do."

♣

Julia looked down at the half-eaten pizza slice that rested on the molded plastic seat beside her in the airport waiting area. "I guess you found lunch without me," Abby was saying, her voice clear through Julia's cellular phone.

"Oh, don't worry about me, Abby. I won't starve," Julia said before taking a sip of her full-calorie Coke.

*Damn Lance Collins.* He had left an entire case of the stuff, and Julia couldn't bear to throw it out. Now she was addicted. Between that and the whole milk she'd been drinking, she was glad to be going on tour. She needed to drop a few pounds, and more than a couple of Lance's bad habits, to distance herself from all the parts of Lance that remained long after he was gone.

Abby carried on. "Well, I'm heartbroken I couldn't see you while you were in town, but you know how it is."

Julia looked at the notebook peeking out of her bag and reassured her editor. "That's fine, Abby. I'll see you on my way back through. Maybe I'll have a draft ready for you by then."

"Jules," Abby protested, "I know you're good, but you're

not Wonder Woman. No one can finish a book and travel and do press at the same time. Just enjoy the trip. And sell lots of books!"

"I will. Thanks, Abby."

"Oh, hey, while I've got you on the line, I should fill you in on some sad news." A tremor of dread rippled down Julia's spine. "Turns out our friend Richard Stone hasn't paid income taxes in seven years."

Julia felt like the jets that were taking off outside. "Really?"

"Really. He's left town completely. I think we've heard the last of Richard Stone."

"Oh, Abby." Julia gathered herself. "That's great. I don't know how to thank you."

"I told you," Abby joked. "Sell lots of books!"

"Okay." Julia laughed. "I'll get right on that."

She hung up the phone, checked the board behind the airline counter, and saw that her layover had been extended by two hours. *Great,* Julia thought. *I'm behind before I even get started.*

She reached for her notebook, knowing that she needed to write, especially if she wanted to truly impress Abby and have an early draft when she came back through New York. But Julia didn't feel like writing. For the first time in her career, she had writer's block. She'd told herself that once she started traveling, the inspiration would flow, but so far all she'd felt had been jet lag and turbulence. Inspiration was like lost luggage, and she traveled on, hoping it would turn up somewhere along the way.

She fumbled in her purse for a pen, but found her deck of cards instead, and couldn't resist laying out a hand of solitaire. The cards fell beautifully into place, so she flew through them, her hands moving without the benefit of her mind, her entire existence on cruise control. Then, as soon as the easy moves disappeared, she heard the words that had been echoing in her head for weeks: *Keep on playing solitaire. . . . Keep on laying out those cards, and then ask yourself when you're Ro-Ro's age if it would have been so awful to put that painting someplace.*

She shook her head, looked away from the cards, and nearly jumped out of her skin when she caught sight of Lance Collins.

# Chapter Twenty-seven

**WAY #96: Let go of your baggage.**
Life is going to be very long and difficult if you insist on carrying items that are better left behind. No matter if it is a nasty breakup or bad job interview, or anything in between, don't let those things drag you down.

—from *101 Ways to Cheat at Solitaire*

Julia thought for a second that her mind was playing tricks on her. But no, there they were. In the lower-right-hand corner of the magazine, staring her in the face, were large, bold letters that read: LANCE COLLINS—NOT JUST A PASSING FAD!

"Ma'am," Julia said as she moved and sat next to the older woman across the aisle.

"Yes, dear?" the woman said in a beautiful Irish lilt.

"May I . . . ?" Julia gestured to the magazine, completely unable to finish her sentence, certainly incapable of walking twenty feet to a newsstand to buy her own copy.

"Why, certainly, dear," the woman said, and handed the

magazine to Julia, who felt her breath catch as she looked down at the black-and-white photo on the cover.

She ripped through the pages until she saw his face again. She looked at the smile that he used to give to her and realized that he was now giving it to America. A pang of jealousy ripped through her, and she began to read.

### LANCE COLLINS: NOT JUST A PASSING FAD

In an all-night bakery in TriBeCa, Lance Collins looks like a lot of other men. Look closer. You might notice his smile first; most people do. Or maybe his gray eyes and dark brown hair. Maybe his large hands and firm grip as he stands and welcomes you to the table. You think you've seen him before, but you just can't put your finger on where. Well, don't worry. In seven months, when the first of his three new blockbuster films hits theaters, his will be a face you won't be able to forget. For now, you remember the pictures of him with a certain self-help diva who shall remain nameless, and you think, again, that he reminds you of someone you maybe had a crush on once. Guess what? You're probably right.

When I met Hollywood's latest "It" boy, a few blocks from where he's just begun shooting a new movie, I had to do a double take myself.

FAD: Thanks for making the time to meet with me. Our readers are dying to learn more about you.

LC: Oh, thanks. It's really no trouble. Glad to do it.

FAD: So, I'm just going to lay this out there. What is your relationship with Julia James?

LC: (laughs) She's a friend. A wonderful person. I wish her all the best.

FAD: Is it true that your relationship was fabricated to boost her sales and launch your career?

LC: That would be kind of hard, considering we never had a relationship and neither one of us ever claimed to. Look, people can believe what they want, what they read, if they're gullible enough. But there's no way a guy like me deserves a woman like that.

FAD: Our female readers will find that hard to believe.

LC: Don't worry, your male readers will know exactly what I'm talking about.

FAD: You're working with A-list people on an A-list project now. How does that feel?

LC: I'm eating better than I have in years, and I'm not tending bar anymore. (smiles) But all joking aside, it feels great. This is what I do. I act. It's great to be acting, period. If you get to do it with the best in the business, all the better.

FAD: What about fame?

LC: (sips his coffee) What about it?

FAD: You saw it growing up with your dad, Academy Award Winner Robert Wells, but you're not using his last name now. Your former agent released that fact to the press, that you come from acting royalty and yet have chosen to use Collins, your mother's maiden name. Why?

LC: (he smirks—ladies, watch out for this man's smirk) I changed my name. My dad is pretty famous. Okay, he's really famous. We look a lot alike, but we're not clones. There's so much nepotism in life, in any career, especially show business. Good or bad. I wanted to make it, but I wanted to do it based on my own merit. That's why the Julia thing never made any sense. Why would I do that to her, put her through that, if all I wanted was a famous name? I had that to begin with.

FAD: You're just friends?

LC: (takes a slow drink of coffee) Yeah.

Lance Collins might have had two stabs at fame the easy way and turned them down, but as the sun rises over Manhattan, I look at the eyes and smile he inherited from his famous father and I realize that like it or not, when America gets an up-close look at Lance Collins, fame is probably going to stick.

Unlike the barrage of reality-show starlets and second-generation wannabes, this "It" boy is destined to be anything but just another fad.

Julia dropped the magazine. The woman looked at her, and then at Lance's picture on the cover. "He's handsome, isn't he, dear?" the woman asked.

"I know him," Julia mumbled.

"Oh, do you now? Tell me." The woman leaned closer, assuming the posture of a confidant. "How well do you know him?"

"I love him," Julia said, surprising even herself.

The woman took in a sharp breath. "What a handsome pair you must make."

But Julia was crying.

"Oh." The woman leaned closer. "What have I said?"

"Nothing," Julia said. "Nothing." She clutched the magazine and started to leave. Then, remembering, she turned to the woman and asked, "May I have this?"

"Well, yes, dear. Of course."

"Thank you," Julia said. She was already running, dodging the commuters in their business suits and the vacationers wearing Hard Rock Café T-shirts and Yankees caps. Her jacket flapped behind her. Her carry-on bag banged against her side, but she didn't care. She just kept running.

♥

The cab turned from Canal Street onto West Broadway. She didn't know where the movie set was, somewhere in TriBeCa. She didn't know if he'd want to see her, probably not. She didn't even know if she had time to see him and make it back to the airport to catch her plane. The craziest thing of all was that she didn't care.

"Lady, I don't know where we're going," the driver said again.

"They're filming a movie down here somewhere," she told him once more. "Just circle around."

"But, lady, that could be . . ."

She slammed a fifty-dollar bill against the partition and

said, "I have a lot of money, and I'm willing to use it to find that set!"

The driver raised his eyebrows and his voice. "Okay," he said. "Your nickel."

They made another turn onto a smaller street, and Julia saw barricades up ahead and a throng of people standing as if they were waiting for something or someone. A cop was directing traffic, trying to make the cab turn around. The driver rolled down his window to speak to the uniformed officer.

"Gotta turn around, folks," the officer said.

"What's going on?" Julia asked from the backseat.

"Street's blocked off shooting a movie."

And with that, Julia tossed money toward the driver and was out the door. She ran the half block between the cab and the crowd. She clutched the magazine, remembering its words: *his famous father's name, fame the easy way.* Fame that had nothing to do with her.

She gripped the magazine and ran harder, pushing through the crowd of onlookers and fans, celebrity junkies, and starving hopefuls. She hoped no one would recognize her as she pushed on through the belly-baring, tattoo-boasting, cappuccino-drinking masses until she reached a very large man in a very small T-shirt who was manning the gap in the barricades.

"I need to see Lance Collins," she said, gasping for breath.

"Yeah, lady. You and every other warm-blooded female in the country." Seeing the issue of *Fad* in her hands, he added, "I love it when the pretty boys are on magazine covers during filming. It makes my life *so fun*."

"But, I know him," Julia said. "I'm"—she lowered her voice—"Julia James."

He looked through a list of names on a clipboard. "Sorry," he said.

"But I'm—"

"Look, lady, I don't care if you're Cleopatra, you don't get in unless you're on the list."

"But I'm a friend of his."

"Then you have his contact info and you don't need to go through me."

"No! I—"

"You're leaving." He nudged her slightly back into the throng of women—younger, thinner, more worldly women who would probably never make Lance break-and-enter.

Julia racked her brain. *What would Nina do? Or Ro-Ro and the Georgias? Or,* Julia asked herself, *Veronica?*

She heard a voice behind her. "Hey, Julia?"

She whirled, praying it would be Lance. It wasn't.

The man was pushing toward her and, although Julia remembered him clearly—it's hard to forget the face of a man who shows up outside a police station with your luggage, airplane tickets, and a running cab—his name was a mystery. She mentally snapped her fingers, trying to remember. She knew he was a member of "New York's thespian underground," but other than that, she was drawing a total blank, so she offered a nice, generic, "Hi!"

"It really is you," he said. Then he pointed to the barriers. "Why haven't you gone in?"

"My name isn't on the list."

"Oh, the list." He gave her a wave. "Come on."

The man guarding the barricades waved at her companion when they approached and said, "Hey, Tom."

*Tom!*

Then barricade man noticed Julia and asked, "Is she cool?"

*Great! I'm at the crossroads of my life, and safe passage depends on being classified as "cool"?*

Tom nodded and said, "You don't recognize her?" Then he added, "She's cool."

*I am?* Julia wondered, but before she knew it, they were inside.

"This is a big set—lots of stars—so security is key," Tom explained as they walked down the closed portion of the street, past trailers and vans and miles and miles of cables. Julia looked around and realized what a far cry that life was from her little farm. She saw millions of dollars' worth of equipment and dozens of hurrying people, and she wondered how long a man like Lance Collins could possibly stay satisfied living in a broken-down house in Oklahoma. She looked at Tom and asked, "He's doing well, then?"

"Are you kidding? Look at this place." He gestured around

him to the dozens of trailers that filled the streets, the crews, the barricades blocking hordes of fans. "He got them to fly me in from California. And when he wraps here, he's going to New Zealand to start the new Peter Jackson. He's on top of the world," Tom said with only the slightest glint of jealousy in his eyes.

Never before had good news made Julia feel so terrible.

"So, what brings you by?" Tom asked.

"Oh, I'm in town for meetings with my editor," she lied. "Then I'm catching a plane to London. I'll be on tour in Europe for a few weeks." She was shamelessly scanning the street, looking for Lance.

"Hey," Tom said. "He's in with Tiffany, but I can get him."

"Tiffany?" she questioned.

"Female lead. Nice girl."

"Oh," Julia said, and tried with every ounce of resolve in her body not to crumble into dust and blow away. "Are they . . ."

Tom looked at her, then he nodded and said, "Yeah, I think so."

"Oh." *That's terrible.* "That's great."

"Why don't you let me go get him?"

"Oh, no," she said, waving off the suggestion. "I've got to catch a plane."

"You sure?" Tom asked, unconvinced.

Julia smiled and said, "Yeah."

"You wanna leave a message?" he asked.

She thought about what she'd say. But of the thousands of

words she'd written in her lifetime, she couldn't imagine stringing a half dozen together to say what she wanted him to hear. She could just say "Hi" like an old friend stopping in out of the blue and disappearing just as quickly. She could take a chance, say the words that had brought her running through traffic and airport security. Or she could say good-bye.

"Actually . . ." She began digging in her bag. "I just need to give him something."

"Can do." Tom nodded and crossed his arms, waiting for his assignment.

She dug into her purse and removed her deck of cards. "Can you give him these, please?"

Tom looked at the ragged deck and seemed to wonder what kind of freak would return something you can buy brand-new for a buck twenty-eight at any corner store. "Any message?" he asked.

Julia shrugged, fighting tears. "Just tell him he broke me of the habit."

"Okay," Tom said, taking the cards without trying to disguise his confusion.

She walked away quickly, certain any more words would betray her. She focused on planting one foot in front of the other as she walked down the Manhattan sidewalk, surrounded by lights and cameras and action, as somewhere in her mind, the soundtrack of her life began to play, and the credits rolled on her romance.

She dodged the busy crews with their bright lights and long

cables. They worked all around her, setting the scene, getting ready to make a perfect movie ending.

Julia always knew it was phony.

In the end, no one goes home with the fairy tale.

# Chapter Twenty-eight

> **WAY #101: Accept the hand you're dealt.**
> True peace comes from accepting what you are—a self-sufficient entity, a deserving individual who is much more than just half of a whole. Sometimes happiness depends on understanding that even a losing hand of solitaire can be a great way to pass the time.
>
> —from *101 Ways to Cheat at Solitaire*

"It's good," Abby said without taking her eyes off the manuscript. "Really, it's good."

There were a few things Julia had picked up from being around professional critics, and one of them was that when a person feels the need to pay a minor compliment twice, they're probably hiding a major criticism.

Julia knew she had it coming. She wanted to blame some of the manuscript's shortcomings on the tight schedule, the challenge of promoting and doing research at the same time, the fact that European stores didn't carry her favorite brand of pen. But those were just excuses. Julia knew too well where the blame belonged.

"It's a marketable book," Abby went on.

"But . . ." Julia prompted.

"Jules, I'm a fan." Abby leaned her small body onto the top of her oversized and impossibly tidy desk. She waved her hand, gesturing to the multimillion-dollar corporation around her. "Everyone here knows it. I've loved everything you've ever published."

*That's what you think,* Julia thought.

"Even those sexy bodice-rippers you wrote way back when," Abby added.

Julia nearly lost her lunch.

"Didn't think I knew about those, did you?"

Julia could do nothing but be honest. "No, I didn't."

"The reason I know is because I happen to be a very big fish in a not-so-big pond. They were good. I agree that they don't exactly 'go' with your nonfiction career, but they're nothing to be ashamed of. Books like that bought my house in the Hamptons." Abby shifted in her seat. "I'm getting off track. What I'm trying to say is that I know you, kiddo. I know how you think and, more importantly, I know how you write. This"—she tapped the manuscript with her glasses—"is good. But it isn't you."

"Well, it's just a draft," Julia hurried to say. "I've still got to polish. You won't even recognize it in a month."

Abby shook her head. "It won't change until you change. I don't know what this Lance Collins business did to you.

Maybe it shook your confidence, opened your eyes to something? I don't know. What I do know is that your first books were fresh. They were fun. But this sounds like work. I don't want to hurt your feelings—it really is good—but it isn't the work of a believer. Do you see what I'm saying?"

Julia nodded, understanding perfectly.

Abby went on. "I could publish this tomorrow and it would debut at number one, and we'd both make a load of money. Or we could sit on it until you get your voice back, and then we'll publish something that we both know is an actual Julia James book. Makes no difference to me. You make the call."

Julia couldn't imagine how this woman could have risen to a position of power in a carpool, much less an entire industry. But, she supposed, there is an inherent strength in kindness.

"What are we going to do?" Abby asked.

Julia thought about it. "I'm going to go home and hang up a picture."

Abby leaned back in her chair. "I don't know what the hell you're talking about," she said, then kicked her feet up onto her desk. "But let me know how it works out."

◆

"Are you sure you don't want me to meet you?" Nina asked as Julia adjusted the grip she had on her cellular phone and looked around the terminal of the Dallas–Fort Worth airport.

"No," she said. "I think I'll rent a car."

"That's ridiculous! I haven't seen you in weeks. Come on,

I'll pick you up. We can go to Hideaway and get a pizza, then go to your . . ."

"No, really, Nina," Julia said, feeling a little guilty, but not so guilty that she was willing to let Nina derail the plan she'd already gotten her heart set on. "I'm looking forward to driving. I've been chauffeured and flown around for weeks now. I want to drive."

"Then you can drive my car."

"I need a little time alone."

"Julia, you've been alone for a solid month and for thirty-four years before that. Don't you think you've had enough alone time?"

Julia thought about it, then said, "I need a little more."

♠

In the rental car, heading home, her headlights sliced through the black, and it occurred to Julia that she didn't need them. She could feel her way, taste it, hear it. All she had to do was follow the flow of the land and the sound of water. It had been a long time since Julia had been homesick, not since she was living in New York, she guessed. Not since before the first book got published and she became famous for being the woman who wasn't waiting for someone to join her at the table. It took another trip to New York and a stranger sitting down beside her at Stella's to convince Julia James that, sometimes, the strength lies in the waiting.

Veronica White was going to come out of retirement. During

the past three weeks, Julia had realized something: If she killed the Veronica in herself, then only the Ro-Ro would survive. Once she'd figured that out, the rest became easy. On the flight from Dallas, she'd pulled out a notebook and felt Veronica's words fly from her fingers.

In her suitcase, she had a dozen home décor magazines and a list of ideas she'd picked up in Paris. She'd given Nina a blood oath that she was serious about the renovation. She couldn't wait to say good-bye to the leaky faucets and cracking walls that had framed the last three years of her life. It was time to start making permanent changes to the house, to every-thing.

She drove down the gravel road in the darkness, ready to begin her grown-up life.

The headlights swept over the house, and she thought, *Home sweet home,* as she parked the car and popped the trunk. She lugged her suitcases onto the porch and struggled with the key.

When, at last, the door was open, she started inside but stopped short. Someone had fixed the door leading into the study. There was a fresh coat of paint on the wall. *Have Nina and the contractors started?* she wondered. But then she saw that new lights had been installed in the ceiling above the fire-place, and they were shining down, accenting her grand-mother's painting, which hung, perfectly centered, above the mantle. She crept closer, wondering who had arranged that surprise. She studied the painting through the lights' glow. Its brushstrokes, the way the oil caught the light. She stepped closer and heard the familiar creak of the floorboards, but another noise as well, something she knew but couldn't pinpoint, something . . .

Behind her, cards shuffled.

Julia turned to see Lance sitting at the dining-room table. He cut the cards, then looked at her. With a sly smirk, he said, "I think it's time you learn how to play gin."

# Epilogue

From EliWinter.com/Julia_James

> **WAY #102: Don't miss a chance to learn new games.**

I am grateful to my publisher, Eli-Winter, for allowing me to write this addendum to *101 Ways to Cheat at Solitaire*. I think it is important to include Way #102, a piece of advice I have taken far too long to offer: There are a lot of games in this world; don't miss your chance to learn them.

A man bought me lunch five years ago. It cost him forty-five dollars plus tax and tip, and in exchange, I received a chicken Caesar salad and a life. From that day on, I had a clear image of myself, a clear purpose for my work. *Table for One*, *Spaghetti and Meatball*, and *101 Ways to Cheat at Solitaire* were the truest things that I could offer to help make the world a better place. I wouldn't change a syllable of any of them, except to add this message.

We wear a lot of labels in our lives, and it's so very easy to be defined by them. We have grown somehow accustomed to thinking of ourselves as a size eight or a size fourteen, as a Capricorn or a Taurus, as single or in love. I was very good at being single—so comfortable on my own that the thought of sharing my life with someone else was quite scary and completely unknown. Thinking of myself beyond that familiar label is the hardest thing I've ever had to do. I've found a way to win at solitaire, but life is full of other games. Someone has come along and offered to teach them to me.

Who would I be cheating if I didn't try to learn?